*BEST*

A chance to read and collect some of the best-loved novels
from Mills & Boon—the world's largest publisher of
romantic fiction.

Every month, four titles by favourite Mills & Boon authors
will be re-published in the *Best Seller Romance* series.

A list of other titles in the *Best Seller Romance* series
can be found at the end of this book.

Sara Craven

# THE DEVIL AT ARCHANGEL

**MILLS & BOON LIMITED**
15–16 BROOK'S MEWS
LONDON W1A 1DR

*First published in Great Britain 1978 by Mills & Boon Limited*

© Sara Craven 1978

*Australian copyright 1978 Philippine copyright 1978 This edition 1984*

ISBN 0 263 74878 2

*Set in Linotype Plantin 10 on 11 pt. 02–0984*

*Made and printed in Great Britain by Richard Clay (The Chaucer Press) Ltd, Bungay, Suffolk*

# CHAPTER ONE

'Lot thirty-four—this fine pair of Staffordshire figures, ladies and gentlemen. Now what am I bid for . . .?'

The penetrating tones of the auctioneer were suddenly reduced to a subdued murmur as Christina quietly closed the dining room door behind her and began to walk slowly down the flagged passage to the rear of the cottage.

It had been a mistake to stay on for the sale. She realised that now. Mr Frith had warned her that she might find it an upsetting experience, seeing the place she had thought of as home for the past six years being literally sold up around her ears. She should have believed him and moved —not merely out, but away. It was only sentiment that had caused her to remain, she thought. A longing to buy just something, however small, from among her godmother's treasures to provide her with a reminder of past happiness.

As it was, the prices that the china, furniture and other antiques were fetching had only served as a poignant and disturbing reminder of her own comparative pennilessness. She must have been mad even to think of joining in the bidding, knowing that she would be up against dealers and collectors.

One thing was certain—the Websters would be only too delighted with the results of the sale. She had seen them sitting together at the back of the room, exchanging smiles of triumph as the bidding proceeded. Everything, as far as they were concerned, was going entirely to plan. It was no good telling herself that they had every right to do as they had done. They had made that more than clear already in every interview she'd had with them. Legally, she had no rights at all, she knew, and morality didn't enter into it.

She walked despondently into the back kitchen. Like everywhere else in the cottage, it had been stripped bare of everything saleable, and the big fitted dresser looked oddly forlorn without its usual complement of bright willow pattern and copperware.

Christina went over to the sink and ran the cold tap, cupping her hand beneath it, so that she could drink. She pressed the few remaining drops of moisture in her palm against her forehead and throbbing temples.

She still could not fully comprehend the suddenness of the change in her life and circumstances. She knew, because Mr Frith had endlessly told her so, that she must think about the future and make some kind of a plan for herself. But what? It seemed for the past six years she had been living in some kind of fool's paradise. And for that she had to thank Aunt Grace, so kind and affectionate in her autocratic way, and so thoroughly well-meaning towards her orphaned goddaughter, but when it came to it, so disastrously vague.

After all, as Vivien Webster had patronisingly pointed out to her, what more could she expect, when she was not even a blood relation? It was a phrase Mrs Webster was fond of using, often with a delicate handkerchief pressed to her eyes, or the corner of her mouth, and if Christina thought it sounded odd coming from someone who had almost studiously held aloof from Aunt Grace when she was alive, she kept that strictly to herself.

Aunt Grace, after all, had been no fool. She had been well aware that she was regarded as a future meal ticket by her niece and her husband, yet it had made no difference, apparently. Her brief will had left everything unconditionally to Vivien Webster, while Christina who had been her constant companion, run the cottage for her with the spasmodic help of Mrs Treseder from the village, and done all her godmother's secretarial work for the various charities with which she was connected, had not even warranted a mention.

Not that she had ever expected or wanted anything, she reminded herself. It had always been Aunt Grace who had insisted that she had seen to it that Christina would be well looked after in the event of anything happening to herself, although she had never specified what form this care would take. She had said so over and over again, especially when Christina had tried to gain some measure of independence by suggesting that she took a training course, or acquired some other type of qualification.

'There's no need for that, my dear,' Miss Grantham would remark bracingly. 'You'll never want, I promise you. I shall see to that, don't worry.'

And yet, Christina thought wryly, here she was without a job, a home or any kind of security—not even allowed so much as a breathing space in her old home to gather her wits and formulate some kind of plan for the future. She gave a little painful sigh and stared out of the window at the small vegetable garden where she and Aunt Grace had spent so many back-aching hours up to the time of that last but fatal illness.

Not for the first time she wondered if Aunt Grace had really known just how ill she had been. Certainly she had robustly rejected all suggestions that she looked tired, and all urgings to rest more and conserve her energy in the months preceding her death. In fact she had seemed to drive herself twice as hard, as if she guessed that she might not have very much time left, and she had driven Christina hard too.

Christina gave a slight grimace. She had a whole range of accomplishments to put in an advertisement—'Capable girl, nineteen, can cook a little, garden a little, type a little, nurse a little ...' The list seemed endless. Yet she had to acknowledge that she was a Jill of all trades and actually mistress of none. Had she anything to offer an employer more stringent than Aunt Grace had been? This was her chief worry.

Up to now, of course, her not always expert services had been accepted, if not always with entire good humour, but she could not expect that a stranger would be prepared to make the same allowances for her.

She had been whisked off to live with her godmother when her own mother, widowed while Christina was still a baby, had herself succumbed to a massive and totally unexpected heart attack. Christina had stayed on at the same school, aware for the first time that the fees were being paid, as they had always been, by Aunt Grace. When she was sixteen, her godmother had commanded her to leave school to 'keep her company' and she had perforce to abandon any idea of further study and obey. Not that it had been such a bad life, Christina thought, sudden nostalgia tightening her throat. She had liked the small rather cosy village community of which Aunt Grace had been so active a member. She had learned to appreciate the changing seasons with a new and heightened awareness, and had come to enjoy the pattern of her year and its traditional festivities without any particular yearning for the discos and parties being enjoyed by her contemporaries.

Keeping Aunt Grace company had not always been easy. Her godmother was an imperious woman belonging to a very different generation. She did not believe in Women's Lib, even in its mildest form, and it was her openly expressed view that every woman needed a man to look after her and protect her from what she darkly referred to as 'folly', though she invariably refused to be more specific.

Her own form of male protection, for she had never married, came in the substantial shape of Mr Frith, her family solicitor, whose advice she followed almost religiously on every problem, except apparently in one instance —that of Christina's future. Mr Frith told Christina frankly after the funeral and the reading of the will that he had tried on a number of occasions to persuade Miss Grantham to alter her will and make some provision for her, but without success.

'She pretended she couldn't hear me,' he told Christina regretfully, and Christina, who had often been subjected to the same treatment herself when presenting Aunt Grace with some unpalatable piece of information, had to sympathise with him.

All Christina could surmise was that Aunt Grace had intended to make provision for her, but had not been able to decide what form it should take. And now, of course, it was too late and there was no point in wondering what this might have been.

It was clear from the very start that Mrs Webster was not prepared to be magnanimous in any way. Christina was merely an encumbrance to be shed as soon as possible, and she did not even pretend a polite interest in the future of the girl who had been her aunt's ward. Christina was allowed to infer that Mrs Webster thought she was extremely lucky to have lived in such comfort rent-free for so long, and that it would do her no harm to stand on her own feet for a change. Nor did she show any great interest in the cottage or its contents. She did not want to give up her life in London for a country existence, and she made it plain she was only interested in converting her inheritance into hard cash as soon as possible.

Christina had hoped forlornly that the Websters might want to retain the cottage as a weekend home, and might be prepared to employ her as a caretaker in their absence, but she was soon disabused of that notion. And when she quietly asked if Mrs Webster knew of anyone who might need a companion to perform the sort of duties that Aunt Grace had demanded, Mrs Webster had merely shrugged her shoulders and talked vaguely of agencies and advertisements.

Mr Frith and his wife had been extremely kind, and had

promised to provide her with suitable references when the time came. They had even invited her to stay with them when it became clear that she would have to move out of the cottage without delay so that it could be auctioned with the contents. But Christina had refused their offer. Perhaps, she had told herself, the Websters had a point and it was time she did try to gain some independence. After all, she couldn't be cushioned against life forever. There were other places outside this little village and outside her total experience, and she would have to find them.

It was taking the first step that was always the hardest, she decided. Her own first step had been a room in the village's one hotel, but she knew this could not be a permanent arrangement. Her small stock of funds would not permit it, for one thing, and besides, it would soon be high summer and Mrs Thurston would need the accommodation for the casual tourists passing through the village on the way to the coast. As it was, the temporary arrangement suited them both.

Once the auction was over, there would be nothing to hold her here. It was an odd sensation. She felt as if a gate had closed behind her, and she stood alone in the centre of an unfamiliar landscape, unknowing which way to turn.

It was a lonely feeling and she felt tears prick momentarily at the back of her eyelids. It had occurred to her more than once that Aunt Grace might have expected her to marry and find sanctuary that way. Certainly she had always been quite encouraging when any of the local young men showed even a random interest in Christina. But such dates as she had had were few and far between. Christina had felt uncomfortably on several occasions as though her escorts were doing her some kind of favour, and she would not have been human if she had not resented this. After all, her mirror showed that she was not unattractive with her long straight fall of honey-blonde hair, and her thickly lashed grey-green eyes. In deference to Aunt Grace's stated preferences, she had never worn extravagantly trendy clothes and she had wondered sometimes whether outsiders considered her dowdy.

Since Aunt Grace's death, it had occurred to her that the attitude of some of the boys who had dated her might have sprung from the fact that they knew how poor her financial prospects were. It was an unpleasant thought, but it had to be faced. Many of the local families were well-to-do and would expect any future daughter-in-law to be drawn from approximately the same financial background and social standing as themselves. They might be kind, but they would not lose sight of the fact that she was only Aunt Grace's companion.

It was a depressing thought and one she did not feel too inclined to pursue. She glanced at her wristwatch. The sale was barely half over as yet, but she thought it might be best if she slipped away. For one thing, she wanted to avoid another encounter with the Websters, who would be bound to inquire in carrying voices if she had managed to find another job yet. Christina sighed. She did not want to have to admit the humiliating truth—that her few diffident applications for posts so far had not even reached the stage of being invited for an interview.

Besides, she still had the rest of the day in front of her. She could catch the afternoon train to London perhaps and go round some of the agencies that Mrs Webster had mentioned. Perhaps in cases like hers, the personal approach was best. Anyway, time was growing short and she had to find some means of earning her living before her small savings ran out altogether. She had to shake herself out of this painful dream world and take up her life again. There was nothing here for her now, and maybe it had done her no harm to be convinced of the fact.

She took one last and rather sad look at the garden and turned away towards the door.

Then she saw that she was not alone and a startled involuntary 'Oh!' broke from her lips. She had not the slightest inkling of any approach, and there was something in the stance of the woman in the doorway that suggested rather uncomfortably to Christina that she had been there quietly for quite some time.

She was not a tall woman, but she had a definite presence, aided by the fact that she was exquisitely dressed in a hyacinth-blue Italian knitted suit. Her shoes and bag looked handmade, and she leaned on a slender ebony cane with a silver handle.

'Miss Bennett?' Her voice was calm and low-pitched with more than a trace of some foreign accent.

Christina hesitated for some reason that she could not herself have defined. Then 'Yes,' she acknowledged in a low voice. 'But I'm afraid I don't know . . .'

'As you say, we have never met.' The other woman smiled slowly, revealing white and even teeth. Yet I assure you, *mademoiselle*, that I do not in the least regard you as a stranger. In many ways, I feel we are old friends.' She gave another faint smile at the bewildered expression on Christina's face.

'I see that I must explain myself more fully. I am Marcelle Brandon, *mademoiselle*. Did your godmother never speak of me to you?'

'Never, as far as I can remember,' Christina told her honestly. 'You—you were a friend of hers?'

She found it difficult to credit in many ways even as she spoke. Aunt Grace had been so thoroughly English—never even journeying abroad as far as Christina knew. It was impossible to imagine how she could have struck up any kind of relationship with this rather exotic-looking stranger.

The other inclined her head. 'We were at school together—also my sister Madeleine. Your godmother never spoke of her either?'

Christina swallowed. 'No. I don't think she ever mentioned her schooldays. It always seemed that any friends she had were here in this village.'

'Latterly that would have been true.' Mrs Brandon shifted her weight slightly and Christina saw with compassion that she was in pain. But it was only a fleeting impression, and when the bright dark eyes met hers again, they were calm. 'Yet we corresponded for many years. I last heard from her some eighteen months ago.'

She glanced around. 'I regret that I am unable to stand for long periods and there does not appear to be a chair...'

'No, everything went for the sale.' Try as she would, Christina could not keep that note of desolation completely out of her voice.

'Then perhaps you know of some more comfortable surroundings where we could talk—where there will not be so many memories, *hein*?'

Christina paused. She could see absolutely no reason why this old friend of Aunt Grace should want to talk to her, apart from sheer kindness of heart in wishing to comfort her in her bereavement. But this she could not quite believe, although she would have been at a loss to explain why. The strongest impression she got from Mrs Brandon was one of cool self-containment. It was hard to imagine her wasting time on meaningless gestures of sympathy. She wondered why she had come now instead of for the funeral, and who had informed her of Aunt Grace's death in the first place. She had had the task of passing on the sad news to Aunt Grace's friends and acquaintances and she knew quite well she had not written to anyone called Brandon. Perhaps Mrs Brandon was here at the auction because she too had wished to buy some last souvenir of her friend, but again this seemed to be out of character.

But why am I saying that? she thought, appalled. I've only just met her. She's a stranger to me. I shouldn't be attributing motives or anything else to her on first meeting.

She smiled over-brightly, trying to compensate for her own guilty feelings.

'There is the place where I'm staying,' she said, a trace of doubt creeping into her voice. Somehow she could not visualise Marcelle Brandon among the faded tapestry covers and mock horse brasses of Mrs Thurston's sitting room at the Bay Horse.

'But that would be ideal,' her visitor said smoothly, scooping up Christina's mental arguments and dismissing them before they could find utterance. 'Perhaps there might also be some coffee.'

'I'm not sure about that,' Christina admitted. 'There'll certainly be tea.'

And tea there was, accompanied by some rather powdery scones. Marcelle Brandon appeared to bear up philosophically under this, but Christina noticed that she barely touched her cup and merely crumbled one of the scones on her plate. Although she had said she wanted to talk, she seemed in no hurry to break the silence that had sprung up between them. She seemed, Christina thought idly, a thousand miles away, her mind fixed on some interior vision, not altogether pleasant. Then she reproached herself for an over-active imagination. After all, this woman had been a close friend of her godmother's. It was natural that she should seem a little withdrawn. It could not be a happy experience for her to be here now, knowing that they would never meet again.

She cleared her throat. 'You were very fond of my godmother, *madame*?'

Mrs Brandon seemed to return with a start to her present surroundings. She lifted one elegantly shaped eyebrow. '*Naturellement*, or I should hardly be here.'

'No.' Christina flushed slightly. Then she took her courage in both hands. 'Forgive me, *madame*, but I don't really understand why you have come.' She swallowed. 'I—I suppose it's none of my business, but . . .'

But the half-expected snub was not forthcoming. Instead Mrs Brandon smiled slightly.

'*Au contraire*. It is precisely on your business that I have come. Your godmother wrote to me when she first suspected she might be seriously ill. She never mentioned this to you? No, I thought not. She was concerned as to what might become of you when she died as she was aware that any financial provision she might make in her will would in all probability be contested in the courts, and this would be both costly and unpleasant for you. Her niece—is it not?—plainly resented you already and would have accused you of exerting undue influence on your godmother if she had made you a bequest as she wished.'

Christina nodded dully. 'Mrs Webster doesn't like me— not that we've met very often. She hardly came near Aunt Grace when she was alive ...' She paused, aware that she might be giving away too much, but Mrs Brandon gave an understanding nod.

'You are very young, *ma chère*—Christina, is it not? And you do not yet fully comprehend the way of the world.'

'If it's the Websters' way, I don't think I want to comprehend it,' Christina flashed back, then bit her lip.

Mrs Brandon laughed and leaned back in her chair, taking a cigarette from her bag and fitting it into a silver holder. '*Bon*,' she approved, a little mockingly. 'I am glad you are not wholly lacking in spirit. You are such a little pale thing. I did not expect ...' She broke off and lit her cigarette. Blowing out a cloud of fragrant smoke, she regarded Christina through half-closed eyes. 'Tell me, *ma chère*, what plans have you made? You cannot, one would imagine, intend to stay here?'

'Oh, no.' Christina shook her head. 'That—that would be out of the question, even if I wanted to. I have to get a job.'

'Very commendable. Have you anything in mind?'

Christina hesitated. It was humiliating to have to admit the truth—that with her lack of qualification she would have to take what she could get and be thankful.

'Because, if not, I have a plan to put to you,' Mrs Brandon continued as if she had not noticed the awkward little pause. 'I myself am looking for a secretary/companion and I think you would suit me very well, if you were willing.'

Christina set her tea cup back on the tray with a hand that shook slightly.

'It's very kind of you, *madame*,' she said quietly. 'But I'm sure I'll be able to find something. I—I don't need charity, however kindly meant.'

'You think I offer charity? Then you do not know me very well. I do not offer a sinecure, my child. I suffer from arthritis, as you have seen, and I am not a patient sufferer— my temper has never been of the sweetest. Also there is the isolation. We have none of the entertainments or amusements that young people of your age seem to expect nowadays—no discothèques or night clubs.'

In spite of herself, Christina had to smile. 'I should hardly miss that kind of thing,' she returned drily. 'The Swinging Seventies seem to have passed me by up to now.' She sent the older woman an inquiring glance. 'You say your home is isolated, *madame*? Where do you live? I gather it's somewhere in France, but . . .'

Mrs Brandon shook her head. 'I have never lived in France. I was born, as was Madeleine, my sister, on Martinique in the West Indies. We both attended a convent school in England, and that was where we met your godmother. When I married, I went to live on Ste Victoire, another island, though not so large as Martinique and belonging to the British. In fact, my husband and his brother, who is now dead, owned the greater part of it, and our family still lives at Archangel.'

'Archangel?' Christina's face was alive with interest. 'What an unusual name for a house.'

'Yes—and the story behind it is also unusual. It is not merely a house, you understand. There is also a plantation. And because so much of it is private property, Ste Victoire has not been developed and spoiled as so many others have been. I think you would like it there.'

Christina swallowed hard, trying to hold on to reality. Was this really happening to her? Was she actually being offered a job on a Caribbean island—something she had never contemplated even in her wildest dreams? But in spite of her inner excitement, a small voice of sanity still prevailed.

'But why me? There must be hundreds of people far better qualified than I am who would give their eye teeth for a job like that?'

'Not as many as you would think,' Mrs Brandon returned. 'As I have said, the island is very remote and has few of the glamorous trappings one associates with such a place. We lead quiet lives in privacy. This is not the Caribbean of the travel posters, I assure you. I should warn you too that there are many dangerous reefs around our shores, and that in stormy weather we are often cut off for weeks on end. We have learned to be self-sufficient, because we have had to be.'

Christina shook her head. 'I still can't really believe this is happening,' she said rather quaintly. 'Nor can I understand why you think I would be suitable. After all, you know hardly anything about me.'

'I know sufficient,' Mrs Brandon said quietly. 'I know from her letters that Grace was most fond of you.' She leaned forward and placed her hand over Christina's. 'Would it make any difference if I told you that it was your godmother's dearest wish that you should come to me?'

'No,' Christina said unhappily. 'Or—perhaps not in the way you might think. You see, *madame*, it is charity after all, and I don't want that. I've got to learn to be independent. It's very kind of you, and I'm sure Aunt Grace had the best of intentions, but I would hate to think I'd been—well—palmed off on to someone ...'

'What is this "palmed off"?' Mrs Brandon's tone was cold and she sat back in her chair again, her brows drawn together in a quelling frown. Her glance chilled Christina.

'You leap to conclusions, my child. If anyone performs a charity, it will be you. A young fresh face to keep me company—young, willing feet to carry messages. You imagine you will not earn your salary? I promise you that you will. There are many lonely spinsters I could choose if I wished to be charitable. But I am a selfish old woman. I wish for someone decorative, and above all someone who will not bore me with a lot of sentimental chatter about past times I have no wish to remember. The young are so impatient generally. They wish the bright lights—the beach parties, and that I cannot offer. But you, I think, have learned the art of patience.'

Christina sat in silence, her thoughts whirling. The temptation to take Mrs Brandon's words at their face value and accept her offer was almost overwhelming. Almost. Yet, at the same time, her pride baulked at the idea of being handed over from one elderly lady to another. Could this be what Aunt Grace had meant when she had told her that she would see she was taken care of in the future? It was galling, to say the least, as if she was being given no credit for having sufficient intelligence or energy to carve out a life of her own.

She could not deny, however, that if she had merely seen the job advertised somewhere, she would have applied for it. A vision rose in her mind of silver sand and palm trees and softly curling surf. It was like having some cherished wish granted by the wave of a wand. Yet Mrs Brandon with her smooth white hair and air of aloofness was far from being the conventional picture of a fairy godmother, she thought wistfully.

'You trouble yourself quite unnecessarily, you know.' Mrs Brandon's ironic voice cut across her inner musings. 'Would it make it more acceptable to you if I specified that the position would be on trial at first—let us say a month on either side. In fact it might be better if you regarded your visit as a holiday at first. You have been under some strain lately, and it may be unfair to press you until you are rested and more relaxed. Well, what do you say?'

Christina hesitated, then gave a deep, sigh. 'What can I say, *madame*? You are too kind. You make it impossible for me to refuse. I don't know how to thank you.'

'Have no fear, my child. I will think of a way.' Mrs Brandon grimaced slightly with pain as she reached for her stick. 'So it is settled, then—a few weeks in the sunshine, and then we can decide on some more—permanent arrangement.'

She rose slowly and carefully to her feet, waving away Christina's proffered assistance.

'Your first lesson, *ma chère*. I do not care to be helped,' she remarked with a bleak smile. 'I shall return to London now. But before I go, I shall settle your account here with the good woman downstairs. You will have the goodness to pack your things this evening and be prepared to join me in the morning, not later than ten o'clock. Of all things, I detest unpunctuality,' she added almost as an afterthought.

'But I'm quite able to pay my own bill here. I do have a little money ...' Christina began. She felt apprehensive suddenly. Too much was happening and too fast. Even Aunt Grace had never taken charge with precisely this *grande dame* air, and it was curiously disturbing, as if she was now merely a puppet, content to dance while Mrs Brandon pulled the strings.

'Keep it.' The older woman's tone was negligently dismissive. 'Or better still, use it to buy some cooler clothes.' She looked with disfavour at Christina's admittedly rather baggy tweed skirt, and the pullover she wore with it. 'What you have seems more suitable for the sub-arctic region rather than the tropics. Choose plenty of cotton—you will find it cooler than these synthetics—and bring a swimsuit.'

Christina's bewilderment grew. 'But I thought—you said there would be no beach parties.'

'Nor will there. Nevertheless the beaches are there to be

used, and I imagine you were taught to swim at school. I
hope that you will look on Archangel as your home, not
your prison.' Mrs Brandon's tone was faintly derisory, and
Christina flushed, feeling that she had spoken foolishly.

As she saw her blush, the older woman's expression
softened a little, and a slight warmth entered her voice.

'Keep your money,' she repeated. 'Allow me to do this
for you as a mark of my affection for your godmother.'

When it was put like that, she could hardly refuse without sounding totally ungracious, Christina thought.

She accompanied Mrs Brandon downstairs and saw her
into the waiting hired car. She hesitated as it drew away,
her hand half uplifted as if her visitor might look back, but
Mrs Brandon did not turn or make any kind of farewell
gesture, and Christina let her own hand drop after a
moment, feeling foolish again.

She went slowly back into the hotel, hardly able to believe the events that had just transpired. In the space of an
hour, her whole life had been turned upside down, and she
felt quite dazed. Mrs Thurston was hovering beside the
reception desk, a series of questions bursting to find expression. She had been impressed by Mrs Brandon's icy air,
and she was clearly and rather unflatteringly amazed when
Christina explained what had brought her to the village.

'Well, there's a thing,' she muttered at intervals as Christina outlined her rather sketchy plans for the immediate
future. 'Well, I hope you're doing right, Miss Bennett, and
no mistake. After all, you've only got her word for it that
she even knew Miss Grantham. Don't you go taking too
much on trust now, even though she does seem to have
plenty of money about her. You be careful. You read such
awful things in the papers nowadays.'

Christina was torn between her own doubts which Mrs
Thurston was voicing up to a point, and the ludicrous picture of the remote Mrs Brandon as a white slaver which
the landlady was obviously enjoying. The doubts won.

There was a good chance that Mr Frith might still be at the sale. He of all people should know whether or not Mrs Brandon was genuine.

The sale was clearly over, and cars were pulling away when Christina trotted breathlessly up. Mr Frith was still there, and she saw with a sinking heart that he was standing beside the Websters' car saying goodbye to them. She hesitated, but in that moment he saw her and beckoned to her, so she had perforce to approach.

'Now then, my dear, where did you vanish to?' He looked her over smilingly.

Christina paused. She had no real wish to discuss this latest change in her fortunes in the hearing of the Websters, so she smiled and murmured something inaudible, hoping they would drive away.

Vivien Webster, however, put her head out of the window and surveyed Christina superciliously.

'Did you want something?' she inquired.

'Just a word with Mr Frith.' Christina, to her own annoyance, felt herself flush.

'I see.' Vivien was silent for a moment, then she said quite gently, 'You will remember that his time costs money, won't you? You can't expect a professional man to continue indefinitely giving you free consultations.'

Her face flaming now, Christina turned to Mr Frith. 'I'm sorry,' she stammered. 'It never occurred to me ...'

'Or to me.' He squeezed her arm reassuringly. 'What can I do to help, Christina?'

She shook her head, trying to back away. 'It doesn't matter. I only wondered ... I mean do you know ...?'

'Oh, for heaven's sake,' Vivien Webster interrupted irritably. 'If you have something to say, say it and get it over with!'

Christina tried to ignore her. 'Did Aunt Grace ever mention a Mrs Brandon to you?' she asked, but before he could reply, Vivien had butted in again.

'The Brandons of Archangel?' she demanded in a surprised tone. 'But of course she's mentioned them. She was
at school with the wives—I forget their names, but they
were sisters and they married two brothers—quite a
romantic story. Why do you ask?'

Christina supposed she could refuse to answer, but it did
not seem worth the trouble.

'Because Mrs Brandon is in England and she has offered
me a job,' she said with a certain dignity.

Vivien and her husband exchanged glances. 'Why on
earth should she do that?' the other woman asked coldly,
after a pause. 'You're even less to her than you were to my
aunt. Have you been writing begging letters to Aunt
Grace's wealthy friends? I do hope not, Christina. It's so
degrading . . .'

'I've done nothing of the sort,' Christina said hotly. Tears
were not far away, but she blinked them back furiously,
refusing to give way to that sort of weakness in front of her
present audience. 'I never even knew of her existence until
today. Apparently Aunt Grace wrote to her when she first
realised she was ill.'

'Well, it seems most extraordinary that she should just
arrive like that,' Vivien declared. 'Was she at the sale?
I'm surprised she didn't introduce herself.'

'She did,' Christina said quietly. 'To me.'

Vivien gave her a hostile look. 'Well, I still don't see
what interest she has in you. I suppose you spun her some
sob story about being destitute. I hope no one sees fit to
remind her that there's such a thing as Social Security.'

Mr Frith touched Christina's arm and she turned to him
gratefully. 'What kind of a job is it that she's offered to
you?' he inquired kindly. 'The name is well-known to me,
of course. I believe Miss Grantham has known both the
Mrs Brandons since her girlhood, but I had no idea she intended to contact them on your behalf. I must say it seems
a godsend under the circumstances.'

'I don't see why,' Vivien interrupted again. 'I can see no need to turn to strangers. Angela Morton is looking for a reliable mother's help again—the au pair stormed back to Sweden yesterday—and I've almost promised her that she could have Christina.'

Christina felt almost sick with anger. She had heard of Vivien's friend Angela before. She had four young children and did not believe in discipline of any kind. If Mrs Brandon had indeed been a white slave trader, she thought furiously, she would still have opted for her rather than the Morton ménage.

She made herself smile, aping Vivien's own superciliousness. 'What a pity you didn't think to mention it to me,' she said with a fair degree of carelessness. 'Then, of course, I wouldn't have agreed to go to the West Indies.'

Vivien gave her a fulminating stare, then sat back in her seat and wound the window up in bad-tempered jerks.

Beside her, Christina heard Mr Frith give a little sigh as their car drew away.

She gave him a wan smile. 'I do seem to have committed myself, don't I?'

'Perhaps that isn't such a bad thing,' he commented drily. 'It isn't easy to find work these days, and this offer seems to have come at just the right time for you.'

'Yes,' Christina acknowledged doubtfully. 'It just seems so odd that she should want to do this for me. I mean, she could just have thrown Aunt Grace's letter away and forgotten about it. Mrs Webster was right, really. I am a complete stranger to the Brandons and they have no obligation to do anything for me. As it is, I don't even have to make up my mind yet about working for her, but can just have a holiday at Archangel.' She repeated the name wonderingly. 'How strange that sounds.'

Mr Frith frowned a little. 'If you're really unsure, Christina, I can always make some inquiries for you,' he said. 'Have you any reason to doubt this lady's probity?'

'Oh, no,' Christina said quickly. 'It seems she's just what she said—a friend of Aunt Grace's. That's really all I wanted to know.' She paused, then held out her hand. 'I shall be joining her in London tomorrow, so I don't suppose I shall have the chance to see you again. Will—will you thank your wife for me for all her kindness.'

Mr Frith took her hand and pressed it warmly. 'I hope everything works out well for you, my dear. It seems your godmother did have your best interests at heart after all. A summer in the Caribbean at the very least. We shall all envy you.' He hesitated briefly. 'If you—should find yourself in difficulties of any kind, you can always write to me. I know it's what Miss Grantham would have wished.'

'Yes.' Christina felt suddenly awkward. 'Thank you for that—and for everything.'

She felt curiously forlorn as she watched his car drive off, as if she had lost her only friend in all the world. And that was nonsense, she told herself robustly. She now had Mrs Brandon, who had come halfway across the world apparently to befriend her, and there would be other people too—at Archangel. People she had not known existed, whom she would meet and learn to know in the weeks to come.

But, strangely enough, as she turned to walk back to the Bay Horse, that thought did not bring in its train quite the comfort that she had expected.

# CHAPTER TWO

CHRISTINA opened the louvred shutters and stepped out on to her balcony into blazing sunshine. She looked down into an interior courtyard of the hotel where gaily coloured loungers surrounded the brilliant turquoise of a swimming pool and gave a little sigh of satisfaction. Mrs Brandon had been angry in the extreme when a delay in their flight to Martinique had meant that they missed the afternoon boat to Ste Victoire, but Christina herself had no regrets. She had not the slightest objection to spending some time in Martinique, even though she had resigned herself to the fact that there would be insufficient time to pay a visit to Les Trois Ilets, the birthplace of the Empress Josephine of France. On the way to the hotel, she had seen a large statue of the great lady and realised how proud the Creoles were of their famous daughter.

Mrs Brandon had retired to her room and had curtly advised that Christina should do the same, but Christina knew that she would never rest. It was all too new and exciting, and her first jet flight had stimulated her rather than induced any signs of jet lag.

It was still very much a flight into the unknown as far as she was concerned. She still knew very little about Archangel and its inhabitants, and her diffident questions had met with little response from Mrs Brandon. One thing she had elicited was that Vivien Webster had been quite right when she had said that Marcelle and her sister had married two brothers. She had also learned that Madeleine Brandon and her husband had both died in a boating tragedy a few years earlier, although she was given no details.

One thing Christina had found out for herself was that

25

Mrs Brandon had not been unfair to herself when she mentioned her temper. After only a day in her company in London, she had learned that the older woman expected any service to be rendered both promptly and perfectly. Otherwise, a thinning of her lips and a slight spot of colour in each cheek signalled storms ahead. She was unfailingly civil to Christina, but various members of the staff both at the London hotel and later at the airport had suffered under the whiplash of her tongue. Christina decided wryly that Mrs Brandon had probably been right to warn her that a job as her companion would be no sinecure, but in some ways this made her feel better about the whole thing. At least, if she stayed, she would feel she was earning her salary, she told herself prosaically.

But her thoughts at the moment were far from prosaic. Life was suddenly too golden, too full of promise for that. It had been real and earnest, and might be again, but now she was free to indulge herself in any fantasies that occurred to her. She could even, if she wished, change into one of the new bikinis in her case and go down to join the sunbathers round the pool, just as if Aunt Grace's rather mousy little goddaughter who had never worn anything more daring than the regulation one-piece swimsuit on the school uniform list had never existed.

Perhaps she didn't, she thought wonderingly. Perhaps all along that had merely been a façade for this strange, excited creature, enclosed in her iridescent bubble of exhilaration. The thought that all bubbles burst eventually, she crushed down with determination, lifting her face almost ecstatically to meet the sun.

One thing was certain. No matter what Mrs Brandon had said, she was not going to spend the rest of the day shut up in a stuffy hotel room. She had gathered from her employer that visits to Martinique were rare, and she was going to make the most of this one.

Half an hour later she was descending the wide stairs to

the foyer. She had changed out of the trouser suit she had worn for the flight, and was wearing a brief scarlet cotton skirt, topped by a white shirt which tied in a bow at the front of her waist, leaving her midriff bare. She had experimented with her hair, tying it back with a ribbon, and piling it on top of her head, but had finally decided to leave it loose on her shoulders, even though, she thought with a grimace, it made her look younger than ever.

She had shopped for her new clothes in London, revelling in the choice offered by the boutiques and department stores. It was such fun for a change to be able to choose things because they were becoming, and not because they were classic styles which would 'wear'. Mrs Brandon, to her surprise, had encouraged her to pick gay clothes and up-to-the-minute styles, but when Christina had mentioned that she was planning to visit the hotel beauty salon to have her hair cut and re-styled, her employer had issued an implacable veto.

Christina supposed rather ruefully that she could have insisted, but it did not seem worth making a fuss over such a relatively unimportant matter. Besides, Mrs Brandon's attitude had taken her aback somewhat. She would have supposed that Mrs Brandon would prefer her new companion to look slightly older and more dignified without a mass of hair hanging round her face, but it proved, if Christina had needed convincing, that her employer was not a woman who could easily be summed up, or whose reactions to anything could be confidently predicted.

She had bought a small guide book at the reception desk, and decided to confine herself to an exploration of Fort de France. Time did not permit very much else, although she would have liked to have taken one of the guided tours to Mount Pelée, and the nearby city of St Pierre which the volcano had well-nigh destroyed over seventy years before.

But Fort de France had plenty to offer in the way of sightseeing. Christina was entranced by the houses with their wrought iron grillework, so redolent of bygone eras when Creole beauties wore high-waisted Empire line dresses, and cooled themselves with embroidered fans rather than air-conditioning. She toured the cathedral, and walked dreamily through the Savane, oblivious of the other tourists and their busy cameras.

The perfume shops on the Rue Victor Hugo lured her into parting with yet more of her direly depleted stock of money, and she could not resist buying a tiny doll in the traditional *foulard* costume of Martinique.

There seemed to be flowers everywhere. Bougainvillea and hibiscus spilled from balconies in a riot of colour, and street sellers pressed bunches of wild orchids and other exotic blooms on her as she walked along. But she refused them smilingly, using her schoolgirl French. It would be a shame to leave them behind to wither and die in the hotel, she thought, and she could not imagine that Mrs Brandon would happily accept the spectacle of her companion boarding the morning boat, weighed down by flowers.

She was beginning to feel hungry and would have liked to sample the reality behind some of the delectable odours that drifted from the restaurants she passed, but Mrs Brandon had made it clear that they would be dining at the hotel in their suite, so she regretfully turned her steps in the direction of the hotel. Or thought she did.

Somewhere along the line, the advice in her little guide book had been misleading, she thought vexedly. Or, more likely, she herself had simply taken a wrong turning. Certainly she had never seen this particular street before, and she should have found herself in the square in the front of the hotel.

Biting her lip, she swung round, staring back the way she had come. Don't be a fool, she adjured herself briskly, fighting a feeling of slight panic. You're not lost. You just think you are. One of the main streets will be just around the corner, and you'll soon get your bearings again.

But the corner merely led to another street, narrower even and shabbier than the one she had just left. The shadows were lengthening now, and the tall houses with their crumbling stucco seemed to crowd in on her disconcertingly. A dog lying on its side in the shade lifted its head and snarled at her, and she crossed the street, her heart beating a little faster, to avoid it.

This is what happens, she scolded herself, trying to regain her confidence, when you overestimate your capabilities as a tourist. The fairy-tale had suddenly degenerated into a nightmare in this grimy and unprepossessing place, and like a child, she found herself wishing desperately for the fairy-tale again—for the silken thread that would lead her out of the labyrinth and to safety, back to the bright streets and the scent shops and the flowers.

Her footsteps slowed as she gazed uncertainly around her. Somewhere in one of the high shuttered houses, a child was crying, a long monotonous drift of sound that played uncomfortably on her tautened nerves. There were other footsteps now coming steadily and purposefully along the street behind her, and she gave a short relieved sigh. At last there was someone she could ask, and surely, even with her limited French, she could make herself understood and obtain directions back to the hotel.

But even as she turned, the halting words died on her lips. There were three of them, youths of her own age or even slightly younger. When she stopped, they did the same. They stood a few feet away from her, their hands resting lightly on their hips, silent, even smiling a little, and Christina knew she had never felt so frightened or so helpless in her life. For the first time since she had left the hotel, she was acutely conscious of the length of leg revealed by her skirt, and the expanse of bare flesh between her shirt and the waistband of the skirt.

It was a war of nerves that was being waged, she thought despairingly, as they stood facing each other, but she didn't know what else to do. Something told her that to make a run for it would be fatal. Besides, where could she run to? They were cutting off one of her lines of retreat, and who knew what might lie at the end of the other.

She tried to drag the rags of her courage around her, lift her chin, bluff them into thinking she was unconcerned, but she knew by the widening grins on their dark faces that they were not deceived.

Someone had once told her that panic affected the throat muscles, making it impossible to scream, and she thought it must be true, because when the hand fell on her shoulder from behind her, the cry that welled up inside her found utterance only as a strangled gasp. The street dipped and swayed suddenly, and instinctively she closed her eyes. A man was speaking in *patois*, his voice resonant, slightly drawling even. The fingers that gripped her shoulder felt like a vice.

When she opened her eyes again, the street in front of her was empty and the silence seemed to surge at her. She turned almost incredulously to look at the man standing behind her. He was tall, his leanness accentuated by the lightweight tropical suit he wore. His hair was tawny, and there were lighter streaks in it where the sun had bleached it. His grey eyes looked silver against his deep tan, and his firm, rather thin-lipped mouth looked taut, either with anger or some other emotion she could not comprehend.

She wanted to thank him, and instead she said inanely, 'They've gone.'

'Naturally,' he said coolly. 'Are you disappointed?'

His English was faultless, without even a trace of an accent, she thought in the few seconds before the meaning of his words got through to her.

'You must be out of your mind!' she flared at him.

'I must?' His brows rose. 'And what about you—roaming the back streets of a strange town? Do your parents know where you are?'

'I'm not a child.' Infuriatingly her voice trembled. 'And I'm here with my employer.'

'Employer?' He studied her for a moment, and a smile touched his mouth that flicked her, unaccountably, on the raw. 'My apologies. I didn't think you were old enough to be a—working girl. But the way you're dressed should have given me a clue, I suppose. What are you—an actress or a model?'

He was laughing at her. He had to be, although she couldn't read even the slightest trace of humour in his voice. Instead, there was a cold cynicism which chilled her.

'I'm a sort of secretary,' she said quickly, trying to still her sense of annoyance, reminding herself that she had to be grateful to him. 'And I ought to be getting back. I'll be missed by now.'

'I don't doubt it,' he said drily. 'Well, Miss Sort-of-Secretary, and what do your duties consist of, precisely? Can you type?'

'A little,' Christina said, her bewilderment increasing with every moment that passed. After all, he had come to her rescue of his own volition. She hadn't even called for help, so why was he behaving in such a hostile manner?

'Only a little? But then I suppose your talents really lie in other directions?'

For a moment, Christina remembered the advertisement she had drafted in her own mind days ago in the back kitchen of the cottage, and a rueful grin lifted the corners of her mouth.

'I suppose you could say that,' she admitted, then cast a distracted glance at her watch. 'Heavens—the time! Can you—would you be kind enough to direct me to the Hotel de Beauharnais? I thought I was heading there, but I must have taken a wrong turning somewhere.'

'What an admission,' he said satirically. 'You know, you aren't running true to type at all.' He put out lean brown fingers and cupped her chin, lifting her face so he could study it more closely. The insolent assurance of his touch unnerved her, and she jerked her chin away.

'Please don't do that,' she said, making a perceptible effort to stop her voice from trembling again. 'I—I don't like to be touched.' She hesitated. 'I know I should have said so before, but I don't know how to thank you for—for coming along when you did. I really was so frightened. If you hadn't been there, I—I can't bear to contemplate what might have happened.'

'You'd have had your handbag snatched,' he informed her mockingly. His smile widened, as her startled disbelieving gaze flew to his face. 'Poor Sort-of-Secretary. Expecting to be another rape statistic when all they wanted was your money!'

Their eyes met and held. To her horror, Christina realised she was near to tears. The shock of her recent experience coupled with this incomprehensible attitude on the part of the stranger who had aided her was having a devastating effect on her emotions. More than anything else, she wanted the refuge of her hotel room.

'I didn't know what to think.' She lifted her chin with unconscious dignity. 'Situations like this are rather new to me. Now, if you could show me the way to the Beauharnais.'

'Just follow the scent of affluence,' he advised sardonically. 'Actually you're not too far away. You want the next left turning, and the second right after that, but unless you know them these back streets can seem like a maze. Next time you want to play tourist, stick to the boulevards. At least the people you meet there will know the rules of the game.'

With a brief nod, he turned away and continued on down the street. Christina watched him go, aware that her heart was thumping in an erratic and totally unprecedented manner. She told herself that she was glad to see him go, to be free of that disconcerting silver gaze and bewilderingly barbed tongue. She was thankful that he had not offered to accompany her to the hotel, she told herself defiantly, and if he had done so, she would have refused his offer.

No matter how odd his manner, his directions were re-assuringly accurate, she found a few minutes later as she emerged into the square and saw the opulent colonial lines of the Beauharnais confronting her. She quickened her steps, instinct telling her that Mrs Brandon's rest would have ended long ago and that her absence would have been noticed.

She crossed the *trottoir* quickly, swerving between the laughing, chattering groups of people making a more leis-urely return to the hotel for dinner, followed by an even-ing's entertainment. For a brief moment she felt envy stir within her. Her time here was so brief, and tomorrow she would set out for a very different existence on Ste Victoire, with no very clear idea what, if anything, she had to look forward to. She shook her head impatiently, tossing back her hair. She mustn't think like that, she chided herself. It was the chance of a lifetime, and she was just allowing the afternoon's experience to upset her unduly. After all, here she was back safe and sound, with only her pride bruised a little—and that was a condition she had learned to live with.

As she approached the hotel's imposing portico, she noticed that a group of tourists had gathered at one side of it, and were obviously watching something that was taking place in the shade of one of the tall columns which decor-ated the entrance.

She hesitated for a moment, then deciding she might as well be hanged for a sheep as a lamb in the matter of late-ness, threaded her way through the group to see what was interesting them all so closely. It didn't at first glance seem to be too impressive. A tall, lanky Negro with grizzled hair was crouching on the ground, tossing what appeared to be chicken bones in front of him. In front of him, a matronly-looking woman with blue-rinsed hair was also crouching, oblivious of the damage the dusty ground was

doing to an expensive suit. As Christina paused, she got to
her feet, brushing her skirt almost absently, an expression of
mingled alarm and delight on her plump good-natured
face. She took the arm of a well-dressed man standing behind her and they moved away. As they passed her, Christina heard the woman say, 'But that was truly amazing,
honey. He knew everything ...' Oh, she thought, as com-
prehension dawned, a fortune-teller.

Momentarily, she lingered, waiting to see who his next
client would be from the laughing jostling little throng
that surrounded him, but no one seemed very willing to
step forward. The man waited, leaning his back against
the column, his calm liquid eyes travelling speculatively
round the group as if there was all the time in the world.
He made no effort to tout for custom, Christina noticed
curiously. With a feeling of anti-climax she began to back
away and to her alarm felt someone grasp her arm.

'Now then, little lady.' A plump, bespectacled man in
brightly coloured sports shirt and slacks beamed at her.
'Why don't you try your luck?'

The people round him agreed enthusiastically and in
spite of her protests, Christina found herself being pushed
to the forefront of the crowd. She was blushing with annoyance and embarrassment. She wasn't altogether averse to
having her fortune told and she knew—of course she did—
that it was all harmless fun, yet at the same time she was
reluctant to take part in what amounted to a public per-
formance. It must be her day for finding herself in situations
that were none of her making, she told herself philosophically as she squatted obediently in front of the fortune-
teller and added some coins to the battered tin at his side.
She didn't know what to do—whether or not to extend her
palm for him to read, but in fact he seemed totally oblivious
of her presence. All his attention seemed to be concentrated
on the small pile of bones he was tossing in his hands. She
waited rather uncomfortably, feeling that she was making a

fool of herself for the second time that day, and that she did not want to be told that she would soon make a long journey and meet a dark stranger. That was the usual jargon, wasn't it?

The bones cascaded to the ground with heart-stopping suddenness and the man bent forward to examine them. There was a long silence, and Christina felt suddenly edgy. Oh, why couldn't he do his spiel and get it over with? she wondered, visualising Mrs Brandon's reaction if she were to emerge from the hotel and find her new companion sitting around in the dust, waiting to hear details of an imaginary future.

'You must take care, *m'm'selle*.' The man's voice, suddenly hoarse and harsh, recaptured her wandering attention. 'I see evil. You must beware—beware of the devil at Archangel.'

Abruptly he rose to his feet, snatching up the bones and the tin cup, and walked off through the crowd, ignoring the disappointed protests that followed him. Christina got to her feet, smoothing her skirt, aware of the curious glances that were being directed at her. Her face flaming, she almost ran to the hotel entrance, the man's words sounding like a warning drum beat in her head—'*Beware—beware of the devil at Archangel.*'

She still had not fully recovered her composure the next day when she set out on the last lap of her journey to Ste Victoire with Mrs Brandon. But, if she was honest, the fortune-teller was not wholly to blame for this. Mrs Brandon had indeed been angry to find that she had gone out—unaccountably so—and Christina had found herself wilting under the lash of her tongue. Nor had a halting attempt to describe her afternoon's ordeal and its strange aftermath led to any softening of her employer's attitude. Mrs Brandon did not hesitate to imply that Christina had asked for everything she had got and more, and when Christina had tried to tell her about the fortune-teller, she had been imperiously waved to silence.

Dinner was an uncomfortable meal, with Mrs Brandon maintaining an icy reserve which boded ill for the future. It was not as if her anger had been roused by concern for Christina and the danger she had been in. It seemed simply to have been caused by the fact that her instructions had not been obeyed to the letter.

Christina was thankful when she could at last withdraw to her own room. She felt unutterably weary, but perhaps predictably, sleep would not come. No amount of logical reasoning could dismiss the chill of the fortune-teller's warning.

She told herself over and over again that he must have an accomplice in the hotel who made it his business to acquaint him with details about guests which he could use. And Mrs Brandon was obviously well-known at the Beauharnais. The very fact that Christina was travelling with her revealed that her destination was Archangel, and the man had simply been trying to give the crowd their money's worth by introducing a touch of drama into a very prosaic situation. It was so simple, when she worked it out. Why, then, couldn't she believe it? She wished that she had been given the trite prediction of wealth and a handsome husband that she had originally envisaged. It would have been something to smile over in the months to come.

Instead, she was facing the journey ahead with a strange reluctance, unable to dismiss the murmurings of inner disquiet. It was not simply her discovery that Mrs Brandon's temper was all she had suspected, and worse—she could have lived with that—but rather all the unanswered questions she had pushed to the back of her mind in the relief of having a job offered to her and some kind of future to look forward to. Again, she found herself wondering why Mrs Brandon had come personally to England to seek her. Her health, after all, was not good—far from it. As well as her arthritis, she seemed to be taking a variety of tiny capsules for other purposes, and Christina could not help suspecting that she had a bad heart. If that was the case, then why had she not appointed some kind of agent rather than put herself to all the trouble of a journey half way across the world?

She would have liked to tell herself that it was compassion and kindness that had prompted the action, but she knew that such a conclusion would merely be an exercise in self-deception.

She was forced, instead, to conclude that Mrs Brandon had some urgent reason for wanting to look her future protegée over in person, although she could not even hazard a guess as to what that reason could be.

But the feeling of elation that had gripped her on her arrival in Martinique was sadly lacking as she stood by the rail of the boat which was taking her to Archangel and caught her first glimpse of Ste Victoire. She was alone, Mrs Brandon preferring to rest in one of the air-conditioned cabins, and so she had no one to influence her first reactions to the place that was to be her home.

It was inevitably a nervous arrival. Christina's heart was frankly in her mouth as she saw how the boat had to edge its way past the crippling reef to get into the calm waters of the harbour, and she remembered uncomfortably how Mrs Brandon had warned her that they could be cut off in bad weather. It was June now, and she had read somewhere that summer was not the pleasantest season in this part of the Caribbean, with the possibility of hurricanes ever-present.

She sighed impatiently. There was little point in thinking like this. She was just making herself miserable. She was letting an absurd prediction, uttered to impress a crowd of credulous tourists, prey on her mind too much. After all, she had suffered none of these qualms back in England, when she could have retracted if she had wanted to. And she had also discovered, on Martinique, that this smiling Paradise could have its darker side, yet it would be foolish to allow this to outweigh all the other considerations. This, after all, was where Aunt Grace had wanted her to be, and she owed it to her godmother at least to try and give this new life a chance.

She lingered on deck as the boat docked, watching with fascination as the gangplank was run out and the freight and few passengers bound for the island began to be disembarked. An opulent car was drawn up on the quayside and a coloured man in a chauffeur's uniform was standing beside it, leaning against the bonnet. Christina knew without being told that this was the transport from Archangel, and she went below to inform Mrs Brandon.

She was surprised and somewhat gratified to receive the beginnings of a wintry smile and even the command to see that all the luggage was collected and taken up on deck was delivered in reasonably amiable tones. Perhaps Mrs Brandon was pleased to be home and would mellow accordingly, she thought optimistically as she supervised the transfer of their cases.

She accompanied the older woman down the gangplank, carefully avoiding any appearance of concern or the offer of help. When they reached the quay, Mrs Brandon stood for a moment, white-lipped and an expression of strain tautening her clear-cut features, then she had herself under control again and was leading the way towards the car.

The chauffeur snatched off his cap and came to meet them, grinning broadly.

'Welcome home, *m'dame*—missy.'

'It's good to be back, Louis.' Mrs Brandon relinquished her cane to him and climbed into the back of the car. Christina watched as the chauffeur, in spite of the sticky warmth of the day, wrapped a silken rug around her feet and legs.

'You may travel in the front, *mon enfant*,' Mrs Brandon

decreed autocratically, and Christina climbed obediently into the passenger seat. It was very hot in the car and she would have liked to have wound down the window, but something warned her that Mrs Brandon liked to travel in the equivalent of a Turkish bath and that she would do well to accept the situation. Anyway, she thought, surreptitiously pushing her hair off the nape of her neck, Ste Victoire wasn't a very large island and they would soon be arriving at Archangel. She began to think longingly in terms of a shower and a cool drink.

The harbour area of the island did not strike her as being particularly attractive—a cluster of whitewashed buildings with corrugated iron roofs, many of which seemed to be in an advanced state of rust. The streets leading away from the harbour were narrow and crowded with every type of traffic. A lot of people, Christina noticed, were riding bicycles, many of them wobbling along precariously with large bundles on their heads or on the handlebars in front of them. Pavement stalls heaped high with exotically coloured fruit and vegetables threatened to spill into the road, and there seemed to be children and animals everywhere. She had to admire the imperturbable skill with which Louis negotiated his route, but she had to breathe a silent sigh of relief when the township was left behind, and they emerged on to a wider, straighter road which they seemed to have all to themselves.

But after they had been travelling a few minutes, Christina realised ruefully that width and straightness were its only attributes. In other ways, it was little better than a dirt track with gaping potholes every few yards, and although Louis restricted the speed at which they were travelling to allow for this, not even the car's luxurious springing could save them from being jolted.

The road began to climb quite steeply after a few miles, and Christina could see the sea again in the distance, a deep fantastic blue merging unnoticeably with the sky. She caught her breath at its beauty, and Louis grinned broadly as he caught a glimpse of her rapt face.

'You wait, missy.'

They were passing through cultivated fields, where people were working. Many of them straightened and waved as the car sped by, and Christina had a vision of Mrs Brandon sitting alone in the back, acknowledging the salutations with a regal movement of her hand, but she did not dare to turn round to see if she was right. She guessed, however, that this was the edge of the plantation that Mrs Brandon had mentioned. The size of it frankly amazed her, stretching away as far as the eye could see, and interspersed with clusters of dwellings, belonging, she surmised, to the plantation workers. It was like a little world within a world and Christina found herself wondering whether she would ever be familiar with all its workings. Everything—the heat, the parched-looking ground, the vivid blossoms on the trees and shrubs that lined the road—seemed so alien somehow after the gentleness of the English countryside. In spite of the neatness of the cultivated acres, bisected by irrigation channels, Christina had a sense of wildness, of a landscape that had not and never would be completely tamed.

She took a handkerchief from her shoulder bag and wiped the perspiration from her forehead and upper lip. The car was running along at the side of the coast now, the road falling away unnervingly to the silver beach far below. Christina gazed longingly at the creaming surf curling softly on to the sands, and imagined the faint salt-laden breeze that would be blowing off the sea. The heat inside the car was beginning to make her head throb, and she was aware of a slight feeling of nausea. Surely the journey couldn't take much longer.

She leaned back against the padded seat, closing her eyes and trying to ignore the frequent lurches as the car coped with the uneven surface of the road. Then, just as she thought she was going to be forced to ask Louis to stop

the car, the ordeal came to an end. The car slowed, turned
sharply and settled on to a surface that felt as smooth as
silk after the horrors of the past few miles. Half unwillingly, she opened her eyes and found that they were travelling suddenly under a cool green arch of trees.

'Nearly home, missy.' Louis' voice at her side was brisk
and reassuring and Christina realised gratefully that her
discomfort had been noticed. She could not repress a feeling of excitement as the seconds passed.

One last, deep bend and the house lay in front of them,
shaded by tall encircling trees. It was painted white, a long
two-storey building with a wide terrace running its full
length on the ground floor and echoed by the balcony with
its wrought iron balustrade outside the upper rooms. In
front of the house formal lawns, and flower beds vibrant
with blossoms stretched away, and Christina noticed that
there were sprinklers at work. The car stopped at the foot
of the terrace steps and Christina saw that a tall woman was
waiting at the front door to greet them. By her dark dress
and spotless white apron, she guessed she was the housekeeper. She waited at the side of the car while Louis helped
Mrs Brandon out. The air was warm and filled with a dozen
pungent scents. Christina breathed deeply, feeling the tension that had possessed her slowly draining away. She
looked up at the housekeeper and smiled rather shyly, but
the other woman did not respond. At closer quarters, Christina saw that she still bore the traces of an earlier beauty,
although her face was haggard now, the cheekbones prom-
inent under the coffee-coloured skin.

'Ah, Madame Christophe.' Her cane firmly grasped, Mrs
Brandon began a slow ascent of the wide shallow steps up
to the terrace. 'Is everything well?'

'Very well, *madame*,' the housekeeper replied in a low
voice. 'There have been no difficulties.'

Mrs Brandon paused on the terrace to regain her breath
and then gestured towards Christina who was following in

her wake with Louis, who was carrying their cases.

'This is Miss Bennett, Madame Christophe. You received my cable?'

'A room has been prepared for her.' Madame Christophe's dark eyes surveyed Christina indifferently. 'Welcome to Archangel, *mademoiselle*.'

Turning, she led the way into the house. The entrance hall was large and square with a floor coolly tiled in blue and green mosaics. Christina saw that the principal rooms all seemed to open off this hall, and glancing up she saw that the first floor also took the form of a gallery. At the foot of the stairs and dominating the hall was a large statue in marble. Christina gazed at this wonderingly. It was a statue of a young man wearing armour and wielding a businesslike-looking spear with which he seemed about to kill some strange winged creature lying at his feet. The young man himself also possessed wings, she saw, a splendid pair, tipped with gold.

'That is our protector, *mademoiselle*—St Michael the Archangel, for whom the plantation is named.' Mrs Brandon's voice was cool and slightly amused.

'I see,' Christina said quite untruthfully.

Mrs Brandon smiled. 'I did tell you there was a story about it, did I not? It dates from the seventeenth century when the first family built a house here and began to grow sugar. It was all slave labour in those days, you understand. Well, one batch of new slaves brought disease with them. It spread over the island like wildfire—like the plague, it was. People were dying like flies. No remedy, no precaution seemed able to check it. So, as a last resort you might say, the islanders turned to prayer and to St Michael—they were all of the Catholic faith in those days.'

'And did it work?' Christina asked. 'And why St Michael anyway?'

'Because when plague had ravaged Italy during the years of the Early Church, the Archangel was said to have appeared on a church in Rome sheathing his sword as a sign that the plague would end.' Mrs Brandon's tone was bored.

'Did the same thing happen here?'

'There was no apparition, but the plague vanished almost overnight. The islanders declared it was a miracle, and since that time the plantation has been called Archangel in honour of St Michael. It is a tradition we have maintained. The statue is very old. It was brought from France as a private thanksgiving by the family.' Mrs Brandon spoke as if she had learned her lines from a guide book of doubtful validity.

They moved past the statue and up the stairs. Mrs Brandon halted when they reached the gallery. 'Show Mademoiselle to her room, Madame Christophe. I am going to rest. Tell Eulalie to bring me a tray of iced coffee in an hour's time.'

Christina followed the housekeeper's erect figure along the gallery and through an archway. This led, she discovered, from the main part of the house to a wing running towards the rear. Two thirds of the way along the wide corridor, Madame Christophe halted before a pair of louvred double doors which she pushed open.

Christina gazed almost unbelievingly at the room within. The walls and ceiling were a warm, vibrant honey colour, but the rest of the decor—carpet, silk curtains and hangings —were in cream. Her immediate impression was that it was all much too luxurious for a hired companion who might not even be going to stay.

'Mademoiselle does not care for the room?' Madame Christophe had noticed her instinctive hesitation.

'On the contrary.' Christina made a little helpless gesture. 'It's the most beautiful room I ever saw in my life. But does Madame—I mean Mrs Brandon really intend it for me?'

The housekeeper gave her a calm, rather reproving look. 'She leaves such details as the allocation of rooms to me,' she said with a faint shrug. 'But I can assure you she would approve my choice. Louis has brought up your cases. I will send Eulalie to unpack for you.'

'Oh, no—thank you,' Christina said hastily. 'I'd really rather do that for myself. I—always have.'

Madame Christophe gave her an enigmatic look, then turned to leave. 'But circumstances change, can they not?' she remarked over her shoulder. 'Perhaps Mademoiselle should also be prepared to change with them.'

The door closed quietly behind her, leaving Christina in sole occupation of her new domain. Her clothes, she decided after a hasty inspection, would occupy about a fifth of the row of louvred wardrobes which occupied the length of one wall. Guests who usually stayed in this room probably brought with them an entire Paris collection rather than two small suitcases. A door in the corner revealed a small but well equipped bathroom tiled in jade green, and for the next half hour Christina revelled in the shower she had dreamed of, then, wrapped in one of the enormous bath sheets provided, padded around putting her clothes away in the drawers and cupboards, and setting out her scanty array of toiletries in the bathroom.

Her task completed, she dressed in a chocolate-coloured denim dress with a low back and a halter neckline, and still barefoot walked out through the French doors on to the balcony. To her left, a graceful flight of wrought iron steps led downwards so that the occupants of the rooms in this wing could reach the garden below without having to go through the house. Certainly, it was a beguiling enough scene that met her eyes. An attractively paved patio lay below, with a long rectangular swimming pool as its focal point. Beyond the patio more lawns spread away to become eventually lost in a tangled riot of greenery and flowering bushes, which Christina guessed marked the limits of the garden proper. Beyond this barrier she could see the sea.

She wanted very much to go down the steps and explore

the grounds—to see if there was a way through the shrubbery to the beach, but she hesitated. After all, Mrs Brandon might send for her, and if she was missing and no one knew where she was this would cause problems. And as if to make up her mind for her, a telephone buzzed sharply in the room behind her. Christina walked quickly back into the bedroom and over to the elegant bedside table and lifted the receiver.

'Hello,' she said. 'Christina Bennett.'

There was someone there, because she could hear them breathing—a light shallow breath as if whoever it was had been hurrying. But they did not speak.

After a minute, Christina said sharply, 'Yes? Who is it, please?'

No one replied, but Christina thought she detected a smothered laugh, as if the alarm in her voice had been registered and appreciated. She felt her temper rise.

'Will you please stop playing games and tell me what it is you want,' she said very distinctly into the living silence, and nearly jumped out of her skin as a peremptory tap sounded on the bedroom door.

She swung round with a gasp, still holding the telephone receiver as the door opened. She was confronted by a girl, not much older than herself. She was dazzlingly lovely with dark hair and eyes, and the same smooth *café au lait* skin as Madame Christophe. In fact, Christina thought instinctively, she was the image of what Madame Christophe must have been like at the same age.

The girl smiled—a formal, perfunctory smile revealing white and even teeth. 'If Mademoiselle would care to descend, there is tea in the library. Or would you prefer me to bring a tray to you here?'

'No—oh, no,' Christina said hastily. 'I'll come down. You —you must be Eulalie.'

'That is so.' The dark eyes surveyed Christina and

widened questioningly as she was holding the telephone receiver. 'Mademoiselle desired something?'

'No—someone phoned me, but they won't answer.' Christina felt foolish.

'May I?' Eulalie held out her hand and Christina with a feeling of faint helplessness handed her the receiver.

Eulalie listened for a moment, then turned to Christina. 'There is no one there now, *mademoiselle*. This is the house telephone. It is easy if one hurries to dial a wrong number.'

'But why didn't they say so?' Christina felt that she had been put subtly in the wrong. 'They just wouldn't speak at all. It was horrid.'

'Mademoiselle must have imagined it,' Eulalie said coolly. 'There is no one in the house who would do such a thing.'

She turned and walked to the door, obviously expecting that Christina would follow her. Christina snatched up a pair of low-heeled sandals in natural leather and thrust them awkwardly on to her feet. She felt gauche and confused. She knew she had not imagined the malice she had sensed at the other end of the phone, but she was at a loss to know what could possibly have inspired it.

As she followed Eulalie's studiedly graceful figure along the corridor towards the main staircase, she searched in vain for some topic of conversation. Her position in the household was ambiguous. At the moment, she supposed she was a guest, but no doubt the staff were perfectly aware that she had come here ultimately to work. Perhaps someone had recognised the difference in the way she was being received, compared with the rest of the staff, and resented it. But who? So far, she had only met Louis and Madame Christophe—and now Eulalie. She could not imagine either of the first two indulging in spiteful tricks, while it was physically impossible for Eulalie to have telephoned her. It was disturbing to realise that she had recognised almost at once that the other girl would be quite capable of the action.

And yet Christina could think of no possible motive—for her or for anyone else.

As they descended the stairs, the tall figure of St Michael, the gilded wings gleaming in the sunlight, loomed up in front of them. Christina paused for a closer look at the statue. Somewhat to her surprise, she saw that the winged creature at the angel's feet was not a dragon as she had supposed at first glance, but seemed to have some human characteristics. It was quite repulsively ugly, she decided, wrinkling her nose.

Eulalie had crossed the hall by this time and was standing impatiently at a door on the other side, obviously waiting for Christina to join her. Christina thrust her hands into the slanting pockets on her skirt and nodded towards the carved figures.

'Do tell me,' she invited with a fair attempt at insouciance, 'who is the downtrodden gentleman?'

Eulalie's eyebrows rose and she spared the statue a cursory glance as if she could not understand anyone taking an interest in such a thing. But before she could reply, another voice broke in. A voice, instantly recognisable, which sent the blood racing into Christina's face and curled her hands into fists inside the concealing pockets.

'Why it's the devil, my sweet. The devil himself.'

She forced herself to turn. He was standing just inside the front entrance. He was casually dressed this time in faded denims and a blue shirt that hung open to the waist, but she would have known him anywhere. Those incredible silver eyes of his seemed to be dancing with unholy amusement as he looked her over from head to foot.

'Who else did you expect it to be?' he said gently.

# CHAPTER THREE

CHRISTINA stared at him unbelievably, unable to break the silence which seemed to drag endlessly between them. Of all the people in the world that she had to find waiting for her on Ste Victoire, he had seemed the most unlikely. She had never imagined, even for a moment, that she would see him again, and she had to admit honestly that she hadn't wanted to see him either. She had tried to be grateful for what he had done for her, yet his whole attitude had made her seethe with resentment when she considered it later. At the time she had been too distressed to consider the implications in his words, but that evening in the hotel, burning under Mrs Brandon's displeasure, they had returned to anger her as she sat in her solitary room trying to read a paperback novel she had brought with her.

He had treated her, she thought, as if she had been tried and found guilty. His whole attitude had suggested that her purpose for being in Martinique at all was dubious in some way. But above all he had underlined all her own doubts and uncertainties, making her feel that she was a parasite, dependent for her very livelihood on a rich woman's whim. Her peace of mind had been precarious up to then, but he had given it a further jolt, and for that she could not forgive him.

'You're very silent, Miss Sort-of-Secretary,' he observed mockingly. 'I hope no further disasters have come your way since we last met. Your honour—and your money—still intact?'

Christina lifted her chin defiantly. His appearance and the way he had strolled in uninvited suggested that he was a regular visitor at Archangel, and she knew it would be more tactful to conceal her hostility, but something in his words flicked her on the raw.

Her glance and her voice were cold and unsmiling as she said, 'Thank you—yes. How kind of you to ask.'

His eyebrows rose. 'A touch of English frost. Perhaps a cup of English tea will thaw it. I presume you are on your way to the library?'

It was on the tip of her tongue to deny it and retreat back upstairs to the comparative sanctuary of her room, but she controlled the impulse, aware that Eulalie was still standing by the library door listening with astonishment to this interchange. If she ran away now, she would simply make herself ridiculous, she thought, and forced herself to walk casually across the expanse of gleaming mosaic. She was acutely conscious all the time that his eyes were upon her.

The library was a charming room, if Christina had been in the mood to appreciate it. It was square and low-ceilinged, with a Persian carpet. Three of its walls were occupied by shelves of books from floor to ceiling. The remaining wall was glass—tall French windows standing open to catch the breeze from the gardens beyond. A cream leather chesterfield with matching deep armchairs had been drawn up in front of the windows and a low table placed in front of them. On this had been placed a tray, complete with silver teapot and hot water jug, and delicate china cups. Christina observed with a sinking heart that the tray had been laid for two people.

She glanced instinctively over her shoulder and saw to her dismay that he had followed her in from the hall and was in the act of closing the doors. He caught her glance and smiled unpleasantly as if he could read her thoughts.

'Milk but no sugar, please,' he said sardonically.

Christina flushed and turned hurriedly to busy herself with the teapot. It was obviously a very old one and very heavy. It made her wrist shake and she found to her annoyance that she had splashed tea into the saucer and on to the tray. She bit her lip, very much aware that her unwanted companion was shaking his head as he contemplated her handiwork.

'That won't do at all, Miss Sort-of-Secretary. You'll have to take some lessons before you pour tea for Tante. She's inclined to be—fussy about these things and make her views known. Or hadn't you noticed?'

Christina set down the teapot with a jerk. One word had registered with her. She moistened her lips. 'You say "Tante". Are you—is she . . .'

'I'm afraid so,' he said too gently. 'I suppose this is as good a time as any for formal introductions. I'm Devlin Brandon—your employer's nephew.'

'I see,' Christina said numbly, after a brief appalled silence.

Devlin Brandon produced a battered packet of cheroots from his shirt pocket and lit one. Those strange silver eyes glittered as he watched her.

'I've obviously been an unpleasant surprise to you,' he commented coolly. 'Would it be any comfort if I said you'd caused a similar reaction in me?'

Her head came up indignantly. 'I don't see why.'

'No?' His smile was abstracted as he studied the glowing tip of his cheroot. 'But then you haven't explained to my satisfaction why Tante should need the services of a—sort-of-secretary.'

'Perhaps you'd better ask her that.' Christina took a firm grip on herself and poured tea into the second cup without mishap. She offered it to him. 'And I wish you wouldn't keep calling me that!'

'I can hardly address you as "Hey you",' he pointed out. 'It wouldn't be civil.'

Christina picked up a plate of macaroons and offered these in turn. 'I wouldn't have thought civility would have been a great concern of yours, Mr Brandon,' she said sweetly, and felt she had scored a victory.

But he appeared totally undisturbed, leaning back at his ease in the armchair, his long legs stretched out in front of him. He was even smiling slightly.

'So the kitten has claws,' he observed. 'I advise you to keep them sheathed. There's only room for one tigress in this particular jungle, as you may find to your cost. And I'm waiting.'

'For what?'

'For you to tell me your name and what you're doing here.'

Christina hesitated. Every instinct urged her to tell him that it was none of his business, and yet how did she know it was not? He was a Brandon after all, and she could not be sure what his position in the family was.

'My name is Christina Bennett,' she said eventually and very stiffly. 'And Mrs Brandon has employed me to be her secretary/companion.'

'Is that a fact?' he said softly.

She stared at him. 'You—you sound as if you don't believe me. Why else should I be here?'

'That's what I'm asking myself.' He drew briefly on the cheroot, then stubbed it out in an onyx ashtray on the table in front of him. 'But at the moment I'm not getting any satisfactory answers.'

Christina returned her cup to the tray with a clatter. 'I think you're being rather ridiculous,' she said sharply.

'Am I?' He gave a twisted smile. 'Now then, Miss—er—Bennett. You've met my aunt. Does she really strike you as the sort of woman with the slightest need for a female companion?'

Christina wound her fingers round each other in her lap. 'I suppose that depends on the kind of duties she expects.'

'And precisely what duties do you foresee yourself performing?' he drawled.

She paused. 'We haven't discussed them in any great depth ...' she began.

He snorted. 'That I can well believe. Tell me, Miss Bennett, have you ever held a similar position?'

'Yes, I have.' Christina faced him defiantly. 'I—I have worked for my—aunt for several years in that capacity.'

'And you feel that qualifies you to work for mine,' he said expressionlessly. 'You are either very naïve, Miss Bennett, or extremely clever. I wonder which it is.'

Christina gasped. 'And you are very insulting, Mr Brandon,' she retorted. 'If your aunt considers my qualifications sufficient, surely that's enough?' She got to her feet. 'If you'll excuse me ...'

'Sit down,' he said curtly. 'I haven't finished with you yet.'

She sent him a glittering smile. 'How unfortunate. Yet I, Mr Brandon, have finished with you. Obviously you find me unsuitable for this post—although I'm at a loss to understand why ...'

'At a loss?' he interrupted decisively. 'My good child, take a look at yourself.'

Before she could move, he had risen to his feet. There was a small table on a graceful pedestal just to the right of the door, with a mirror in an elaborately gilded frame hanging just above it. Devlin Brandon took Christina by the shoulders and turned her forcibly to face this mirror. She was shocked by her own reflection—dishevelled hair, flushed cheeks and blazing eyes. She looked like a wild thing, and it was all the fault of this—creature whose fingers were bruising her flesh with their grip. He was holding her against him, and she could feel his skin against her bare back. A weird shiver ran through her, and she struggled to release herself.

'Be still,' he ordered curtly, 'and just ask yourself what possible companionship a girl of your age and appearance could offer a woman like my aunt.'

'Perhaps, Mr Brandon, she doesn't feel quite ready for the scrapheap yet,' Christina fired back. 'She wants someone young about her—she told me so.'

'And you were so fired by the thought of a glamorous life in the Caribbean that you leapt at the job, naturally.'

For a moment, she was tempted to tell him the truth—to confide in someone all the doubts and fears that had beset her, but she crushed it down. If that was what he wanted to think, let him, she thought savagely. Why should she care?

'Of course.' She managed a careless laugh. 'Who wouldn't? But don't think for one moment that I was misled. Mrs Brandon pointed out all the disadvantages to me.'

'And all the advantages—what did she say about them, if anything?' He let her go, and turned away with a weary gesture, walking over to the window and staring out at the gardens.

'They speak for themselves,' she returned defensively. Her shoulders were tingling from the pressure of his hands, and she moved them protectively under the straps of her dress.

He glanced at her over his shoulder and she was chilled anew at the lines of bitterness and cynicism that stamped his face.

'Perhaps they do at that—even for a child of your age. It must take something to persuade you to shut yourself up here in this forgotten world with an autocratic old woman who has yet to be convinced that slavery has been abolished.'

'That's an abominable thing to say about anyone,' Christina said, her voice shaking. 'And about your own aunt . . .'

'Doesn't it fit in with your romantic notions of plantation life? Or did you visualise us all sitting round on the terrace sipping Planter's Punch in happy amity?' He shook his head. 'Don't be deceived by the name, Miss Bennett. It's no Paradise and there are no angels living here.'

She was thankful for the sudden opening of the door. She imagined it would be Eulalie. But it was not.

He was, she decided later, her own age or even slightly younger. His good looks were breathtaking—black hair and dark, glowing eyes, and a mouth with more than a hint of sensuality in its full lower lip. He was dressed for riding, his clothes immaculate, his boots highly polished.

He said directly to Christina very charmingly, 'I'm too late—you've had tea, and I did mean to be back. Please forgive me. I'm Theo Brandon.'

His eyes went past her and narrowed slightly as if he was displeased.

'Hello, Dev.'

Devlin Brandon gave him a dispassionate nod. He said, 'What's this strange passion for tea, Theo? It didn't used to be one of your failings.'

Theo shrugged, his eyes going frankly to Christina. 'I just wanted to welcome our guest.'

'Guest?' Devlin's eyebrows rose. 'I understood she had come here to work.'

Theo gave an impatient gesture. 'Oh, I daresay Grand'-mère will find her something to do if she gets bored, but the plan is for her to have a complete rest in the sun.' He sent Christina a sympathetic glance. 'She's had rather a tough time lately—a family bereavement.'

'I see.' Devlin's breath was expelled in a short, harsh sigh. 'In which case I could have saved myself quite a lot of trouble.' He walked briskly to the door, then paused. 'When Tante has recovered from the journey, you can tell her, if you will, that a deputation from the Island Committee would like to see her—at her convenience, naturally.'

'Do you think it will ever be convenient?' Theo said with a faint grin.

'Probably not, but I was asked to pass on the message.'

Theo sat down on the arm of one of the chairs, flicking at his boot with his riding whip. 'And will you be a member of this deputation?' he inquired softly.

'Of course.' He turned to leave, without sparing another glance for Christina. Her temper rose. This man could do with a lesson in ordinary manners!

'Goodbye, Mr Brandon,' she said clearly and very sweetly.

'I understand the sentiment, but it's a little extreme,' he flung back at her over his shoulder. 'No doubt we shall see more of each other—during your holiday.'

Not if I can help it, Christina thought, smouldering with fury as the door shut behind him. She found Theo regarding her with a curious expression, and flushed slightly.

'Do you find him attractive?' Theo asked with what she thought was deliberate outrageousness.

'No, I don't,' she snapped, then paused, guiltily, realising that they must be related. 'I—I'm sorry. I didn't mean ...'

'No,' he said, and he was laughing. 'Don't spoil it. Your natural reaction was perfect. Devlin would be really put down if he knew. He regards himself as being quite a lady-killer, you know. Women generally seem to find him irresistible. What has he been saying to upset you?'

His bone structure was pretty near flawless, she found herself thinking bewilderedly. He would have been beautiful if it hadn't been for that very positive air of masculinity.

'Oh, nothing very much,' she said, striving to maintain her precarious poise and hoping that he was not aware of her struggle. He seemed very sophisticated for his age. 'We —we'd met before, you see.'

He looked up at her as if he was startled, frowning a little. 'When was this? Does Grand'mère know?'

'No,' Christina admitted. 'I did try to tell her, but she was rather angry with me at the time, and she didn't want to listen.'

Theo smiled, but rather abstractedly. 'Poor Christina— I may call you that?—did she give you a hard time?'

Christina shook her head constrainedly. 'I'm—used to elderly ladies.'

'Well, I'm not angry with you, I'm all agog. When did

you meet dear Cousin Dev, and what did he do to annoy you?'

Christina bit her lip. 'As a matter of fact, he was—very kind,' she was forced to admit. 'He came along quite by chance when I was on the point of being—mugged, I suppose, or something worse—in Martinique yesterday. There were three of them, but when he came, they just—vanished.'

'And were you very frightened?' Theo asked gently. He was smiling again, and his eyes were very brilliant as they held hers.

'Yes—terrified.' Christina relieved those tense moments in the back streets of Fort de France with a shudder. 'I didn't know, you see, what was going to happen.'

'And then along came dear Cousin Dev like Sir Lancelot!' Theo threw back his head and laughed joyously. '*Dieu*, I wish I'd been there!'

'He didn't behave in the least like Sir Lancelot,' Christina retorted hotly. 'His attitude was most unpleasant. He treated me as if I was'—she paused and a phrase of Aunt Grace's floated into her mind—'no better than I should be.'

'Oh?' Theo watched her speculatively through his long lashes. 'Did he try and get you drunk—or did he just offer you a night of sin aboard his boat?'

'Nothing of the kind,' Christina said stiffly. 'And I didn't even know he had a boat.'

'Oh, but he has—an absolute beauty. I'm wildly envious. But you'd better be careful, sweet Christina. I'm told it's the setting he usually uses for his seductions—that or his beach cabin.'

'I'm really not very interested in Mr Brandon's amatory exploits,' Christina said coolly. She gave Theo an uncertain look. 'Did you say he was your cousin?'

'I call him that.' Theo gave a negligent shrug. 'He's actually my uncle—but I'm sure he wouldn't appreciate it if I started addressing him as such. I might do it, though, to punish him—for being unkind to you.'

'Please, no!' Christina was appalled. 'He—he just doesn't approve of my being here, for some reason. Perhaps when he sees that I can work with Mrs Brandon, his attitude will change.'

'Did he know who you were in Martinique—when he performed his daring rescue?' Theo inquired.

'No.' Christina shook her head. 'In fact he gave the impression he thought my employer was a man.'

'How very piquant.' Theo's eyes danced. 'And so he comes sailing peacefully home to find you here. He must have been most disconcerted.'

'I don't really see why. After all, I was expected. My room was ready, and you obviously knew I was coming.'

'Grand'mère sent a cable, naturally, but Dev wouldn't have seen it. He doesn't live at the house, you see.'

'Oh?' Christina was conscious of a feeling of profound relief. Having to share the same roof and meal table with a man whose every remark seemed barbed had not been an enticing prospect. But maybe now she would not have to see anything of him after all.

'You're glad?' Theo's voice, faintly teasing, intruded on her thoughts and she coloured.

'I have no right to be anything of the sort,' she said frankly. 'I ought to remember that he did rescue me.'

Theo yawned slightly. 'Well, don't let it keep you awake,' he advised. 'It may not have been quite the daring deed it seemed at the time. They were quite probably friends of his, and that's why they made off in such a hurry. Dev keeps some pretty peculiar company at times, and his own past doesn't bear looking into. There was even a time when people said he should have been christened Devil instead of Devlin.'

The room seemed to perform a sudden, sickening dive and Christina felt herself totter on legs that were too weak to support her. When she regained her control, she was

sitting on the chesterfield being urged by Theo to put her
head down on her knees.

'I'm sorry.' She put her hand on her forehead. 'I—I'm
still getting acclimatised. It must be the heat . . . I think I'll
go up to my room for a while.'

'That's a good idea.' Theo sprang to his feet, and placed
his hand under her elbow to assist her. 'Lie down for a
little while and you'll soon feel better. I think Cook is
laying on something special for dinner tonight in your
honour, and it would be tragic if you weren't well enough
to come down.'

'Oh, but she shouldn't,' Christina exclaimed in distress.
'I'm here to work, after all. I really am.'

Theo's hand felt warm and solicitous on her arm as he
guided her to the door. 'Of course you are,' he said sooth-
ingly. 'But there'll be plenty of time for that. Grand'mère
wants you to get to know us, to enjoy yourself.'

He would have accompanied her up to her room, but she
assured him she could manage, and he stood at the foot of
the stairs watching her go up.

When she reached the gallery, she turned and smiled
down at him a little uncertainly. He held her eyes with his
for a long moment, then lifted his hand with infinite grace
to his lips and blew her a kiss.

Her cheeks hot, Christina turned suddenly away. Theo
possessed altogether too much charm, she told herself warn-
ingly. She would do herself no good at all if immediately
on her arrival at Archangel she was to embark on a flirtation with her employer's grandson.

She tried to rest, but sleep eluded her. Her head whirled
with a multitude of disturbing impressions, and foremost
of these was the warning she had received from the fortune-teller. '*Beware of the devil at Archangel.*' At least now,
she knew who the devil was and had decided for herself,
even before his identity had been revealed, that he was

someone best avoided. His own overt hostility had taught her that.

If it hadn't been for that, she thought, it could have been quite easy to rationalise what had happened. The fortune-teller had known that she was accompanying Mrs Brandon as she had worked out previously. Therefore he would also know of Devlin Brandon and his reputation—and the nickname that had been bestowed on him and would naturally have woven these elements into his prediction to give them weight. It was a perfectly acceptable explanation for everything that had happened—so why could she not wholly accept it?

It was because there had been something so strange in the man's manner—as if he had been genuinely alarmed by what he saw, or claimed to see, in the chicken bones. And then he had disappeared, even though there was still a crowd of potential clients waiting.

She had already dismissed the notion that Devlin Brandon might have hired the man himself in order to frighten her off. It was obvious he had had no idea who she was when he met her on Martinique, and Theo had confirmed that he had no means of knowing about her appointment until he had arrived at the house that day. Besides, it was a strange sort of contempt, but not menace, that she seemed to detect in his attitude.

He had decided that she was a parasite preying upon his aunt's good nature, she told herself bitterly, and wondered why that bitterness should also contain a trace of despondency. Surely she was not going to let his opinion trouble her? He knew nothing about her or the circumstances in which she had come to Archangel.

She closed her eyes firmly, trying to dismiss the image of that tanned, utterly cynical face from her mind. She would indeed beware of him, she told herself, and with the thought came once more that soft, troublous shiver as she seemed to experience again the hard grip of his hands on her skin and that fleeting contact with his warm body.

She sat up suddenly, pushing her hair back from her face, a feeling akin to panic seizing her. Where was her imagination leading her? She was thinking like a hysteric. She had been touched by men before—she'd even been kissed with varying degrees of enthusiasm and had responded, or not, as the mood took her. Why then was she reacting like this? Almost dazedly she recalled that she had told Devlin Brandon on Martinique that she did not like to be touched. What had possessed her to say such a thing? Yes, she'd been frightened, but not witless. Had she, then, been granted some curious foreknowledge of what this man could make her feel if he chose?

With a little cry she turned and flung herself down on her stomach, burying her face in the pillow and pressing her hands over her ears as if by this means she could shut out the clamour of her thoughts.

If she had to indulge in erotic daydreams, she thought fiercely, then why couldn't she focus them on Theo, blessed with far more than his fair share of devastating good looks and charm? But she knew the answer to that question almost before it was formulated in her mind. Theo, for all his veneer of sophistication, was still a boy. Devlin Brandon, on the other hand, was all man and had probably been so since his cradle.

Stop it—stop it! she raged at herself. It was useless to think in that way, and what was more, it was dangerous too. He was her enemy, and he despised her. She must never lose sight of those facts.

There was a tap at the door, and Eulalie appeared.

'Madame is awake and asking for you,' she announced without preamble.

'I see.' Christina scrambled off the bed and reached for her dress. 'Can you show me where her room is?'

The other girl shrugged. 'I cannot be too long. I have work to do,' she said abruptly.

'I won't be a minute.' Christina stepped into her dress and closed the zip, aware as she did so that her slender figure was being rather contemptuously assessed by Eulalie, whose own body was built on gracefully voluptuous lines. Christina tried to appear unconscious of her regard as she donned her sandals and ran a comb through her tangled hair. 'I'm ready,' she said, turning away from the mirror. Eulalie did not reply, but led the way out of the room and along the corridor to the main gallery.

Mrs Brandon's suite led directly off the gallery, Christina discovered. It consisted of a large bedroom, charmingly furnished in the Empire style in shades of blue and white, with an adjoining bathroom and small sitting room, in which the main item of furniture seemed to be a baby grand piano. A small brocaded sofa with gilded legs had been drawn up to the window, and here sat Mrs Brandon, already dressed for dinner in royal blue chiffon, occupied with some embroidery. An inlaid table had been placed at her side and on this reposed a small silver bell, and a crystal decanter of pale sherry with two glasses.

Mrs Brandon looked round and smiled as Christina knocked and entered.

'Sit down, *mon enfant*. You are rested now?'

Christina smiled and agreed. It seemed the easiest thing to do.

'I should have changed for dinner—I'm sorry,' she apologised, looking down rather ruefully at the chocolate-coloured dress.

'It is of no moment. It is hardly likely that you would be *au fait* with our ways on your first evening.' Mrs Brandon inclined her head graciously in acknowledgment of the apology. 'Besides, the little frock is quite charming.'

Christina was slightly embarrassed by the compliment. Why were all the Brandons quite so overwhelming, she wondered, and would she ever get over this feeling of inadequacy? Determinedly, she took herself in hand. It was her turn to be admiring. Mrs Brandon's needlework was exquisite.

'Thank you.' The older woman's smile was tinged with melancholy. 'I have much to be thankful for. At least my hands still work for me as they always did.'

Christina bent her head sympathetically. It must be agonising, she thought, for such a proud, independent woman to find herself the victim of a crippling disease like arthritis. She found herself wondering at the same time why Mrs Brandon did not travel to America or Europe and take advantage of the latest treatments.

Mrs Brandon folded her work and placed it on the table.

'You may pour some sherry,' she directed, nodding towards the decanter. Christina complied, although dry sherry was not a particular favourite of hers. However, she had to acknowledge that some form of stimulant would be welcome.

Mrs Brandon accepted the glass from her and held it up. '*Votre santé*,' she said kindly. 'Tell me, Christina, what are your impressions of Archangel? Do you think you will be happy to settle here?'

Christina did not know how to reply and took refuge in a barely audible murmur which appeared to satisfy her employer.

'I realise it is early days yet for you to decide such a thing, but at the same time I want you to know that you may consider this as your home for as long as you wish, *ma chère*.'

'You're very kind, *madame*.' Christina sipped at the pale liquid in her glass, feeling rather taken aback. 'I—I promise I'll do my best to—carry out your requirements.' If and when I know what they are, she added silently. Now seemed as good a time as any to introduce the subject. 'Perhaps you'd like to tell me when you wish me to start my duties and precisely what they will be.'

Mrs Brandon waved a hand on which a huge diamond glittered like living ice.

'There is plenty of time for that. For the moment, rest and enjoy yourself. You have, I believe, already met my grandson?'

It seemed a totally casual question, but Christina found herself tensing. She set the glass down carefully on the table. Had someone seen and reported that lighthearted farewell pantomime of a kiss in the hall? She knew that she was blushing faintly and kicked herself mentally for her lack of poise.

'Yes,' she made herself say neutrally. 'He—he came in while I was having tea.'

'So he told me,' Mrs Brandon remarked. 'You seem to have made a lasting impression on him, *mon enfant*.'

Christina looked up startled. 'I would hardly say that, *madame*,' she returned carefully. 'Perhaps boys of his age are particularly impressionable.'

'Of his age?' There was a distinct and disconcerting lessening of Mrs Brandon's benign air. 'He is only a few months younger than yourself. In fact, in appearance—with your hair on your shoulders like that—you seem the younger of the two.'

'Yes.' Christina knew she had to tread carefully. 'But they do say—don't they?—that girls mature much earlier than boys of a similar age.'

'Maybe.' Mrs Brandon's tone was short. 'I have not been acquainted with many young girls, so I am unable to give an opinion. Do you find Theo—young for his age?'

'Oh, no,' Christina hastened to assure her. 'He seemed quite sophisticated—a man of the world.'

'Hm.' Mrs Brandon appeared mollified, she saw with relief. 'It is true he has lacked for young company in the past. I am relying on you, my dear, to rectify that to some extent. You will be ideal companions for one another.'

Christina swallowed. 'But I thought I was to be your companion, *madame*,' she said at last, aware of how feeble the protest must sound.

'Do not take me quite so literally, *mon enfant*.' Madame

gave a slight frown. 'I am not suggesting that you are to work for Theo. I am merely telling you—if you need such assurance—that you are free to accept any invitations from him that he may see fit to make.'

Christina was blushing again, more hotly this time. 'Thank you, *madame*,' she managed weakly.

Mrs Brandon gave her a shrewd glance. 'It embarrasses you that my grandson should find you attractive?'

'No.' Christina gave a tiny shake of her head. 'He doesn't exactly hide his feelings. But since you ask, I must admit I'm surprised that you don't mind him going out with— the hired help. After all, I'm little more than one of the servants here and ...'

'You are my guest and the goddaughter of my old friend.' Mrs Brandon's eyes were suddenly glacial. 'We will speak no more, if you please, of hiring or of servants. You speak as if we were still living in the last century.'

Christina bent her head. 'I'm sorry,' she said. 'But my position here seems so ambiguous ...'

In spite of herself, an inward vision rose in her mind of scornful silver-grey eyes in a tanned face—a harshly drawn mouth that sneered at her as a parasite.

'You seem unduly sensitive about it,' Mrs Brandon chided her, but she seemed to have recovered at least some of her good humour. She put out her hand and gave Christina's cheek a slight tap. 'We shall have to teach you to relax, *ma chère*. You are so tense, so lacking in confidence. Now, ring the bell, and we will go down to dinner.'

In spite of her disturbed emotional condition, not helped by the fact that Theo hardly took his eyes from her during the entire meal, Christina enjoyed her dinner of *calalou*, a Creole soup delicately flavoured with herbs, followed by delicious stuffed crab with rice. The fresh pineapple served for dessert provided a refreshing contrast. Coffee, dark and aromatic with thick cream, was served in what Mrs Brandon referred to as the *salon*, a large and rather formal room furnished in shades of gold and ivory.

While Theo and Mrs Brandon occupied themselves with a rather desultory game of piquet, Christina wandered round the room studying the pictures and ornaments on display. As well as the expected family portraits of long-dead Brandons, executed with varying degrees of competence, there were also a number of paintings of the Impressionist school that she suspected were valuable originals, including a probable Renoir.

Her tour of the room complete, she felt at a loss for an occupation. She would have liked to have gone for a stroll in the grounds, but she suspected that Theo would immediately offer to accompany her, and she wasn't sure how she felt about that. She still felt that her original instinct not to embark on a flirtation with him was probably the right one, although she had no real objection to the idea of being shown the plantation and the rest of the island in his company—but preferably by daylight, she decided.

'Do you like music?' Theo's voice spoke close to her ear, and she jumped slightly.

'Very much, although I don't play an instrument myself,' she returned.

He walked over to an imposing antique cabinet and opened it, revealing a comprehensive built-in stereo unit and a large collection of records.

'What do you like?' He motioned her over to look through the records. 'It is all classical music, I'm afraid. Grand'mère thinks "pop" is an abomination. If you are dying for some dance music, there is a night club of sorts in Port Victoire. We could go there one evening, if you like.'

The invitation was casual enough to be acceptable, she decided, and she could not pretend it was unexpected, so she smiled constrainedly and thanked him.

'Oh.' Looking over his shoulder, she saw one of her favourites. 'Debussy—*La Mer*.'

He wrinkled his nose slightly, but put the record on the turntable.

'You don't care for it?' she asked.

He shrugged. 'It is a little placid for me. Debussy never saw one of our storms, that's for sure.'

'Take care, Theo.' Mrs Brandon, who was playing a complicated form of patience, glanced up. 'You will make Christina nervous.'

Theo looked at Christina, his eyes dancing and his brows slightly raised.

'Oh, I would think it would take more than that, Grand'-mère,' he said softly.

The music had been an unexpectedly soothing conclusion to a strange day, Christina thought later as she went up to bed in Mrs Brandon's wake. Theo had been obviously disappointed at her departure, and she was relieved that her employer had not suggested that she remain downstairs to keep him company.

Her room was quietly welcoming. Someone had switched on the shaded lamp at the side of the bed, and turned down her bed.

She grinned faintly. 'If I'm not careful, I could get to enjoy all this luxury,' she thought.

That was the nub of her problem, of course. It was not hers to enjoy. She was entitled to nothing here. She had come prepared to work for Mrs Brandon, and if no actual job transpired, then she would leave. She had meant what she had said back in England. She did not want charity, however well meant, nor would she accept it. She had to earn a living, and she must not allow herself to become too dependent on the sheltered, comfortable background at Archangel.

When she got to bed, she found that sleep still evaded her. She was over-tired and over-stimulated, she thought, and wished that she had opted for the stroll instead of the music after all. Fresh air might have had the required soporific effect.

After tossing and turning restlessly for some time, she got out of bed and put on her housecoat. She walked over to the window and opened the louvred shutters which closed off the balcony. It was much cooler now, she thought, looking up into the velvet sky where a huge golden moon swam. The air was full of strange scents and sounds—the exotic perfume of frangipani, the chirping of the ubiquitous cicadas. She drew a deep, incredulous breath. It was all so totally alien to anything she had ever experienced. No English night sky had ever looked like that. No English night had ever filled her with quite the same inexplicable yearnings, or the same sweet melancholy. It's a lovers' moon, she thought, and immediately deprecated her own fancifulness.

She turned with a little stifled sigh to go indoors and paused, her attention arrested by a movement below. The figure that emerged from the shadows into the blaze of moonlight was instantly recognisable, although the discreet dark uniform dress and white apron had been replaced by something that clung revealingly to every curve of her body. It was Eulalie, moving with the swaying grace that seemed to be an inherent part of her. As Christina watched, she skirted the swimming pool and walked rapidly over the lawns beyond in the direction of the shrubbery. Although she made no actual attempt to keep herself hidden, there was, at the same time, something strangely furtive about her movements, as if she had no desire to be observed. Once she turned and glanced back at the house as if to reassure herself that no one had seen her go and Christina froze, although she knew she could not be seen from that distance.

She walked slowly back into her room and unfastened her housecoat, tossing it over the dressing stool. Eulalie was plainly going to meet someone. Perhaps it was a lover's moon for her too, she thought with an odd pang which did not lessen in the slightest when it occurred to her that the fact that the girl was sneaking away from the house to meet him indicated that he did not live at Archangel. And as she lay alone, with the moonlight streaming over the bed, she found herself wondering why she was so sure that Eulalie was going to meet Devlin Brandon—and why she should be concerned anyway even if this was so.

# CHAPTER FOUR

CHRISTINA slept restlessly that night and woke the following morning with vague memories of wild and disturbing dreams. She felt drained of energy when she first opened her eyes, but no one could remain depressed for long with warm and brilliant sunshine spilling into the room through the shutters.

A tap on the door signalled the arrival of Eulalie carrying a tray with fruit juice, freshly squeezed, some warm rolls and a pot of coffee. Christina felt embarrassed as she sat up. She had never had breakfast in bed before unless she was ill and it seemed wrong to be waited on in this way. Judging by the mutinous curve of Eulalie's mouth, she was not entranced by the situation either, and her reply to Christina's shy 'Good morning' bordered on hostility.

When she had gone, Christina glanced at the small alarm clock she had brought with her from England. It was still quite early, she saw. Mrs Brandon had warned her the previous evening that she was a late riser, so Christina felt quite justified in regarding the next hour or two as hers alone.

Her breakfast over, she found a pair of jeans and a sleeveless tee shirt and showered and dressed. Her room tidied and her bed made, she made her escape down the garden stairs leading from the balcony and found herself wondering as she walked across the springy grass why the word 'escape' had occurred to her. She was free to come and go —of course she was. Never more so, in fact. At home with Aunt Grace the day's work would already have begun.

As she approached the tangle of flowering shrubs and trees, she saw that a path had been trodden deep into the shrubbery and guessed this was used as an unofficial short cut to the beach. The air was heavy with the hum of bees and other insects, and in the distance she could hear the whisper of surf breaking on an unseen shore.

She hurried down the path, avoiding the roots which protruded from the beaten earth to trip the unwary, and bending her head to escape tangling her hair in the low-hanging branches. It was a narrow path, and the crowding bushes seemed to stretch ahead like a dark, green tunnel where even the ever-present sun could not penetrate. Blossoms, leaves and thorns brushed her body and caught at her clothes as she passed through and ahead of her a splash of brilliant colour told her that her goal was near.

A moment later she stood on silver sand sloping gently down to the creaming water. There might have been no one else in the world, she thought, lifting her face appreciatively to the sun. The only sound was the cry of a bird, and the constant hiss and suck of the tide. Shading her eyes, she could see far out where the great breakers crashed and lost their force on the reef in a tall flurry of spray. But inside the reef, the sea was comparatively calm. Tomorrow she would bring her bikini and swim, she decided. She slipped off her sandals and walked down to the water's edge barefoot, revelling in the warmth of the small waves that curled round her feet, soaking the bottoms of her jeans. She began to walk along the beach, stepping in and out of the water as the mood took her. The faint breeze lifted her hair, making her feel fresh and invigorated—erasing the last vestiges of her restless night.

Perhaps life at Archangel would prove to be much more than just tolerable after all. In her present mood, she felt that she could cope with anything, even unwanted advances from Theo. She found herself smiling at the thought. What had happened to that rather shy girl in England who had been made to feel grateful for a man's attention, however slight? She was probably flattering herself. Theo undoubtedly had a number of girl-friends, in spite of his grandmother's remarks about his rather solitary existence. There was altogether too knowing a look in his eyes for him to have led a completely monk-like existence, and Christina decided that what Mrs Brandon did not know, she could not possibly be expected to grieve over.

Where Christina was concerned, he probably could not resist the impulse to flirt with her, merely because she was there—another moth to be drawn to the brightness of his candle-flame. Besides, if she was honest with herself, Theo was not really her type, despite his attraction. She was quite certain about this, even if she had not yet formulated any definite idea as to what her—type might be. And she was also quite—quite sure that Devlin Brandon did not come anywhere near this vague ideal either. On the contrary, she thought with a curl of her lip.

She was so immersed in her own thoughts, her ears filled with the sound of the sea, that she wasn't aware at first of the muffled drumming sound behind her. And when it did impinge on her consciousness, she couldn't place it first of all. Then with a faint shock, she realised that it was the drumming of a horse's hooves coming along the beach.

She glanced over her shoulder, half resentfully, regretting the loss of her solitude, and tensed. There was no mistaking the tall figure who sat the big black horse as if he was part of it. He wore no shirt and the upper part of his lean, muscular body was deeply tanned. His tawny hair gleamed in the sunlight like a bronze helmet. For one helpless moment, Christina registered the almost magnetic appeal of his sheer masculinity, and then she was running up the beach, her feet sliding in the softer sand, intent only on reaching the comparative sanctuary of the garden beyond.

He was following her, she realised with a sense of desperation, redoubling her efforts. She slipped, wrenching her ankle with a force that brought a cry of pain from her lips, and sank down on to the sand in a huddle of misery, nursing her injured foot.

Devlin Brandon brought his horse to a sliding, snorting standstill and swung himself lithely from its back. He looped the reins loosely over his arm and approached Christina on foot.

'Are you quite insane?'

She did not have to look at him to know he was blazingly angry. She was angry with herself. What a fool she had been to run away like that! She had simply given way to the sort of childish impulse that should have been behind her for ever. Her only excuse was her total reluctance to face him again, and now she could not even remove herself from the scene with dignity.

She tried awkwardly to stand, but collapsed wincing as soon as she tried to put any weight on her ankle.

Devlin Brandon hooked the reins over a substantial piece of driftwood and squatted beside her. She kept her eyes resolutely down as his fingers explored her ankle, trying not to flinch from their warmth on her skin. Even his most impersonal touch was disturbing, she thought with dismay.

'I shall be all right in a minute,' she told him frigidly.

'I'm glad you think so.' He got up dusting the sand from his hands. 'That ankle is beginning to swell—I think you've sprained it slightly. Anyway, it needs a cold water bandage. I'll take you along to the cabin and fix it up.'

'No!' She was shocked by her own vehemence. 'I—I mean—thank you. It's very kind, but I really will be fine. If I can just rest here for a few minutes.'

'Stubborn little bitch, aren't you?' he said almost conversationally. 'I know it must be gall and wormwood to you to be beholden to me again, but you have very little choice. And I promise to confine my interest in your somewhat underdeveloped body to your ankle, if that's what's worrying you.'

She gasped with fury. As his hand reached out to help her up, she bent her head swiftly and sank her teeth into it. He swore and snatched his hand away examining the bright red crescent of marks in his flesh. Christina sat quite still, numb with horror. What had possessed her to do that? she wondered. No matter how barbed his remarks, such behaviour was unforgivable. She glanced up at him, words of apology trembling on her lips, and saw that he was smiling.

'So you bite,' he remarked laconically. 'What a pity it had to be in temper.'

The apology shrivelled unsaid and her face flamed. 'You —you——' she began chokingly.

'Swine?' he supplied kindly. 'Bastard? Sticks and stones, my child. And don't let's play name-calling. For one thing, I'd probably win, and for another it's a boring game for grown-ups. I'll teach you some much better ones—when your ankle's better.'

'You'll teach me nothing!'

'Not even some manners?' Before she could prevent him, he had picked her up bodily and carried her over to where his horse stood patiently waiting. 'This is the second time I've had to come to your assistance, and I can't say your gratitude has been exactly overwhelming.'

He tossed her up into the saddle and gave his bitten hand a pained look before untying the horse and mounting behind her. They began to move off along the beach. Christina sat rigidly upright. She tried to concentrate on her throbbing ankle in an effort to ignore his proximity, but it was impossible. Although he made no attempt to touch her, his arms were round her nevertheless, holding the reins, and his warm body was only an inch or two from hers. If she relaxed even for a moment, there would be actual physical contact between them, and she knew with utter conviction that for her own peace of mind that was something she had to avoid at all costs. She shrank in-

wardly at the thought. It was shameful that she could feel
like this with a man she disliked as much as she did Devlin
Brandon. And it was doubly shameful when he had made it
abundantly clear that her unwilling physical attraction was
not reciprocated. What had he called her? Underdeveloped? Her face burned again.

They were rounding a small headland now, leaving the
bay below the house behind them. Another long expanse of
beach faced them and on the far side of it Christina could
see a building—a large, rambling single-storey shack, under
the shelter of the cliff. Beyond this, a small rather primitive
jetty extended into the water, but there was nothing primitive about the sleek lines of the boat tied up at it. It was a
large powerful-looking cabin cruiser, the paintwork spotless and gleaming. As they approached Christina could
make out the name painted on the hull, *Moon Maiden.*

She was not used to horses and she felt jolted and shaken
by her unexpected ride. Her ankle too was hurting quite
badly now, and she was almost thankful when Devlin dis-
mounted and lifted her out of the saddle. He slapped the
horse on its rear and it threw up its head and cantered off
up a path leading away from the shore.

'Why did you do that?' Christina tried her foot gingerly
to the ground.

'The horse is stabled at Archangel,' he said. 'It knows its
own way home and Marc will see to it for me.'

'I see,' she said, but she didn't. He didn't live at Archangel—presumably this shack was the beach house Theo
mentioned—yet he appeared to have the run of the place
and his pick of the livestock. And the thought came un-
bidden to her mind—did he have the pick of the women
there too?

'Can you walk?' For a moment he watched her tentative
efforts, then swept her up into his arms and walked with her
up the rickety wooden steps to the door.

Her instinct was to struggle, but reason prevailed and

she remained silent and passive in his embrace. Her first confused impressions were of a big room, cluttered but essentially clean with a scrubbed board floor enlivened by a few brightly coloured rugs. There was a long low studio couch heaped with cushions, and to her surprise, at the far end of the room, under a row of windows she noticed a serviceable-looking work bench holding some strange bulky objects covered by cloths.

She was so intrigued that she did not notice he had carried her through a doorway into the bedroom, and by then it was too late to protest. He grinned maliciously as if he could read her thoughts as he dumped her unceremoniously on the bed.

She stared back defiantly, daring him to say anything edged, and after a minute he vanished, presumably to fetch water and a bandage. Christina studied her ankle. The bruise was coming up already and it was quite swollen. It was a relief, if she was honest, to lie on the bed and not have to risk standing on it, but she would much have preferred to have been on her own bed at Archangel. Restlessly she looked round the room. It was not as large as the living room, and she guessed the whole shack had originally only contained one room and that this one had been devised by throwing up a simple partition. A beaded curtain hung over the doorway. The furniture was simple in the extreme, much of it looking as if it had been knocked together by hand. There were a number of bookshelves all solidly filled and, of course, the bed on which she was lying. A double bed.

She was still registering the implications of this when Devlin returned carrying a bowl of water and a first aid box.

'Roll up the leg of your pants,' he ordered, setting the bowl down on the floor beside the bed and pulling forward a wooden stool to sit on. 'Hurry up,' he added impatiently as she hesitated. 'Or I'll do it.'

Hastily she complied, aware of his sardonic grin.

'You really meant it when you said you didn't like being touched,' he commented when the task was completed. 'I'm afraid you'll just have to grit your teeth and bear it for a moment or two. There's no way I can get a cold compress on that ankle without touching you.'

She had to grit her teeth right enough, but not for the reason he supposed. He was gentle, but the fixing of the pad soaked with cold water and subsequent bandaging were not among her most comfortable experiences. Yet when it was over, her ankle felt better almost at once under the firm strapping.

'Thank you,' she said awkwardly.

'That must have hurt more than the sprain itself.' The silver-grey eyes mocked at her, and she flushed defensively. Devlin held out his hand. 'Try and stand on it.'

She accepted his assistance and got to her feet. It still hurt, but it would bear her weight with the support of the strapping he had put round it.

'It's fine.' She moistened her lips. 'I—I'd better be going.'

'Just as you please.' He turned towards the doorway. 'There's some coffee on the stove if you'd like some.'

'I'd better not—I may have been missed by now.'

Eyebrows raised, he glanced down at the watch on his wrist. 'At this hour? You've got to be joking. But run away, if it makes you feel better.'

'It's not that,' she began stiffly, but he cut in.

'What else is it, then? Would it reassure your maidenly scruples if I swore a solemn oath that I have no designs on your spotless virtue?'

Her colour heightened. 'I never imagined for one moment ...'

'And a pure mind along with everything else. Doesn't being perfect all the time become rather—restricting, Christy, my sweet?'

She glared at him. 'You twist everything I say,' she

accused recklessly. 'And my name is Christina.'

'Most of the time it is, I agree.' His eyes went over her with a slow, comprehensive appreciation that made her feel warm and oddly breathless. 'All very sweet and proper and slightly old-fashioned. But when you're sandy and barefoot, and your hair's all tangled because you've just climbed off my bed—then you're Christy.'

'How—how dare you!' Her voice shook.

'You'll find I dare a great many things,' he said coolly. 'There's a spare comb in that top drawer over there, if you want one. I'm going to see to that coffee. Join me when you're ready, if you want.'

She stared after him with frustrated fury. He always gave her the feeling she had made a fool of herself in some way. Why did she allow herself to rise to his baiting quite so easily? she wondered miserably. But in her heart she knew the answer. She had never met anyone quite like him before, and even in that first brief meeting he had disturbed her to the core of her being. The fortune-teller's warning had been fully justified, she thought, biting her lip. She did indeed have to beware of this man—the devil who was tormenting her in subtle ways she had never even guessed at.

She went slowly over to the chest of drawers and paused. Even with his permission, she felt an odd reluctance to rummage through his things to find the comb he had offered. There was an implied intimacy in such an action that she felt she should avoid at all costs. She glanced perfunctorily in the mirror and tried to reduce the worst of the tangles with her fingers. She looked—different, she thought. The sun and wind had put more colour than usual in her face, and her eyes looked strangely bright. She glanced rather doubtfully down at herself. The jeans fitted her closely, and the rather skimpy top clung to her slight curves as if it loved them. She tugged at it tentatively, wondering if there was some way of making it less revealing, then stopped, vexed with herself. She was over-reacting. There was no need for all this concern. Hadn't he said himself that he had no designs on her?

She turned away and walked out through the beaded curtain into the living room. Devlin was at the far end, busying himself with a coffee pot and mugs, and he glanced round as Christina entered. She hesitated, the aroma of the coffee suddenly beguiling in her nostrils. That breakfast she had enjoyed suddenly seemed to have been a long time ago and when he held a brimming mug out to her, it was churlish to refuse. So she accepted it with a murmured word of thanks and sat down on the edge of the studio couch. For a few moments she was tense in case he came to sit beside her, but he seemed content to prowl about the room, sipping at his coffee.

It gave her the opportunity to study the room more closely. It had a casual comfort that she had not encountered up at the house and which had an appeal all its own. But it was essentially a masculine apartment. There was a rack of guns on one wall, and a clutter of serviceable-looking fishing equipment against another. There were no signs of female occupation even on a temporary basis.

She cleared her throat of a slight huskiness. 'Have you lived here long?'

'For the past four years—since my parents died. This was their place—their retreat if you like. They built the landing stage for their own boat.'

Christina glanced at him, startled. She had forgotten for a moment that he must be the son of Mrs Brandon's sister Madeleine who had died with her husband in some kind of accident at sea. She wondered if it was painful for him to be reminded of the fact, but his enigmatic expression gave her no clue.

'And you live here alone?' Now what had possessed her to ask him that? she wondered despairingly as he sent her an amused glance.

'What an improper question,' he said lightly. 'You surely don't expect me to answer it.'

Her face flaming, Christina bent her head over her coffee mug.

'Besides,' he went on, his tone hardening slightly, 'I'm quite sure that my aunt—or someone—has already dropped you a hint about my wicked lusts and other depravities. I assumed that's why you took to your heels when you saw me this morning. On the other hand, it may have occurred to you that running away can be a very provocative thing to do.'

'I certainly didn't mean to be provocative.' She tucked an errant strand of hair back behind her ear with fingers that trembled slightly. 'Perhaps it was simply that I didn't want to talk to you—or anyone else. I was enjoying being alone.'

'That's a strange admission from a professional companion.' He stood looking down at her. 'Or have you decided to forget about that particular piece of fiction?'

'It happens to be fact,' she said tautly. 'I'm sorry that you can't accept it as such. But even if I do have a liking for solitude at times, it won't affect your aunt. I shan't neglect the duties she's paying me for.'

'That's a Christina statement,' he said lazily. 'And I don't doubt the sincerity behind it—or its truth. My aunt wouldn't allow you to neglect her. But you stick to your guns, little one. Keep telling yourself that you've been brought here to be a companion. Only don't try telling me.'

'Why won't you believe me?' she stared up at him.

'Because I know my aunt—have known her for thirty-four years,' he said. 'She's a single-minded lady, and companionship never figured very highly on her list of requirements before—not for herself anyway.'

She set down her mug and gripped her hands together tightly in her lap.

'There has obviously been some rift between you both,' she said. 'I don't know what it is—and it's none of my business anyway. But she is my employer and has been kind to me, and I owe her some loyalty. Maybe you're right and she doesn't need a companion. But she pretended she did so that I wouldn't feel it was charity she was offering. She knew I needed a job and she gave me one for the sake of an old friendship, and I . . .'

She broke off, aware that he was staring at her as if she had gone quietly mad.

'I'm beginning to wonder if we're talking about the same person.' He was frowning and his eyes were intent. 'What are you talking about—an old friendship?'

Christina swallowed. 'I've never had a proper job before,' she said. 'I used to live with my godmother—Miss Grantham. I called her Aunt Grace, but really we weren't related. She—she died some weeks ago, but when she knew she was ill she wrote to Mrs Brandon and—I think—asked her to—look after me. Hence the offer of a job, and that's why I'm here,' she added in a rush.

He seemed almost not to have heard her. 'You were Grace Grantham's goddaughter?'

'Yes,' she answered, bewildered. 'Why, do you—did you know her?'

'I've heard my mother speak of her,' he said curtly.

Light dawned on Christina. 'Yes, they were all at school together, weren't they—your aunt, your mother and Aunt Grace?' She bit her lip. 'But I never knew of your aunt's existence until she came to England to find me. You must believe that.'

His mouth curled sardonically. 'Oh, I believe you, for what it's worth. But it doesn't alter a thing. The best thing you can do, Christina, is get back to England—and that's a friendly warning.'

'I don't need any warnings from you, friendly or otherwise,' she burst out. 'And I can't go back to England yet. I have no money . . .'

'God, what a mess,' he said quietly. He turned away and walked across the room to the open door and stood looking around.

'Then it's my mess,' she said with a kind of dignity. 'I—I know things won't be—easy, but I owe it to Mrs Brandon to—try at least to fall in with her wishes.'

He turned on her and she shrank from the blaze of fury in his eyes.

'Then if that's what you feel—stay, and take what's coming to you. Perhaps Tante made the right choice after all. Just don't come crying to me when things get rough.'

She got clumsily to her feet, wincing a little as she put too much weight on her injured ankle. Her voice shook. 'You're the last person in the world I'd turn to—ever, Mr Brandon. I'm sorry to have put you to so much inconvenience in the past. I'll keep my distance from now on—and that's a promise.'

Trying not to limp, she walked past him to the door. But she was halted before she could reach the refuge of the sunshine. His hand closed with startling suddenness on her arm and she was jerked round to face him.

His voice was quite dispassionate. 'That being the case, here's something to remember me by.'

His arms pulled her closer, pinning her against him in a lingering intimacy that set every nerve-ending in her body quivering. She tried to struggle, but she was helpless against his strength. And then his mouth took hers.

None of the tentative kisses that had come her way in the past had prepared her for this—ravishing of her mouth. His approach was utterly sensual, dark, deep and dangerous. And because he was angry with her, there was an element of brutality as well. A strange tidal race of sensation seemed to be sweeping through her body, destroying the instinctive defences which her total inexperience should have provided. Somewhere inside herself was a stranger whose existence she had never guessed at, with needs she had been unaware of. A stranger whose lips parted under his willingly —too willingly, and whose arms stole up over his bare shoulders to lock round his neck, her hands tangling in his tawny hair.

When her swimming senses subsided and coherent thought returned, she found she was leaning against him, her face buried against the warm brown skin of his chest, hair-roughened and slightly salty under her mouth. His hand was stroking the nape of her neck, and his lips and tongue were exploring her ear.

'Christy,' he muttered, his voice husky but with a note of laughter just below the surface. 'Honey girl. Bite me now.'

His words restored her sanity. With a little cry, she tore herself free, her face burning with shame.

'You—you devil!' she choked passionately, and oblivious of her injured ankle, turned and fled.

She was hobbling quite badly by the time she reached the garden stairs to her balcony. Her feet were sore too. She had not been able to find the sandals she had left on the beach after hurting her ankle. The carpet felt soft and comforting under her bare soles as she padded across the room and lowered herself on to her bed, closing her eyes.

She still couldn't believe it had happened. Where was her self-respect that she could permit a man she hardly knew and heartily disliked to kiss her like that? She pressed her hand to her mouth as if to wipe away the memory of his possession. She had few doubts as to why he had done it. It was simply another way of demonstrating that he despised her. And she had fully justified his contempt by— falling into his arms like that. That was what hurt so much: the knowledge that while she had been in his arms, nothing else mattered—as if time had been suspended.

And if she had not come to her senses in time—what then? Might she still have been with him now—in his arms, in his bed—blind and deaf to everything but the cravings he had aroused in her?

Beside the bed, the phone rang sharply. For a moment she hesitated. If she answered it and there was nothing again but that eerie breathing silence then that would be the last straw.

It rang again, and that decided her. She picked up the receiver. 'Hello?'

'Christina?' It was Mrs Brandon's voice, abrupt with displeasure. 'This is the third time I have rung for you. Where have you been?'

'I've been for a walk.' Christina sat up, pushing her dishevelled hair back from her face. 'I—I'm sorry. Did you want me?'

'Come to my sitting room at once, please.' The other receiver was replaced with something of a slam.

Christina slid off the bed, looking down at herself in consternation. She could not present herself to Mrs Brandon in this condition. That would be adding insult to apparent injury. It occurred to her, with a wry twist of her lips, that her holiday in the sun had been of remarkably brief duration.

She changed quickly into a vivid yellow skirt, and added a sleeveless black silky top with a scooped neck. She gave her hair a swift, hard brushing, then went along the corridor, trying not to limp too obviously.

Mrs Brandon was sitting very upright on her small sofa, her embroidery in her hands. She glanced up rather coldly as Christina tapped and entered, then she saw the bandaged ankle and her attention was arrested.

'You have injured yourself, *mon enfant*.'

'I was on the beach and I twisted my ankle.'

'I see.' Mrs Brandon's gaze went back to the bandage. 'You have had training in first aid, perhaps?'

'No.' Christina could hear the awkwardness in her own voice. 'I—I met your nephew on the beach. He was—good enough to strap it up for me.'

'Indeed?' Mrs Brandon said very calmly. 'That was— most obliging of him. And not for the first time either. Theo tells me that you also met Devlin in Martinique?'

'Yes.' Christina felt her colour rising. 'Though I didn't know who he was then, of course.'

'Of course,' Mrs Brandon agreed in an absent tone. She was silent for a moment, then she gave a little sigh. 'I am in a difficult position, Christina. Yet I feel that I am now responsible for you in the same way as your godmother was, so I must warn you.'

'Against—Devlin?' Christina could feel the betraying colour burning in her face—could see Mrs Brandon noting it, assessing it. The older woman nodded.

'My sister's child,' she said, and there was a world of sadness in her voice. 'She was the only one who seemed to have any influence on him at all—who could restrain this —Brandon wildness. To give him credit, I believe his affection for her was genuine. Certainly I have never known him exhibit any similar emotion towards anyone else.'

Christina sat very still, her hands clasped tightly together in her lap.

'Once the—parental restraint had gone,' the cool voice continued, 'he abandoned any pretence of responsibility towards the family name. He left this house, in spite of all our persuasions—at that time my late husband was still alive— and installed himself in that—hovel on the beach. He gave up any active involvement in the running of the plantation and became—what is that phrase—a drop-out. He now supports himself on the income from the money he inherited from his parents and subsidises himself by—wood-carving.' Mrs Brandon's voice was icy with scorn.

Christina's mind ran back to the work bench she had noticed in the living-room of the beach-house.

'Is he good at it?' she asked unthinkingly.

Mrs Brandon gave her a look of surprised *hauteur*. 'Of what concern is that? He seems to find a ready market for his work. But it is hardly a fitting occupation for a Brandon of Archangel. His duty lay here—in helping me prepare Theo for his inheritance.'

'I don't quite understand . . .' Christina began.

Mrs Brandon sighed again. 'It is all quite simple. My

husband and his brother were twins. My husband was the older by half an hour, and therefore inherited Archangel when his own father died. In fact he and his brother Carey became partners and ran the plantation together. In the course of time, Carey met my sister Madeleine and married her. At the wedding, I met my husband—we were married the following year. We all lived here together and for a while life was very good. The difficulties began later.'

'Madame,' Christina said uncomfortably, 'is there really and need to tell me all this? It's none of my business and . . .'

'I should not have embarked upon it if I did not feel it necessary.' Mrs Brandon resumed her embroidery, her eyes fixed on the minute stitches she was taking. 'You are one of the family now, *ma chère*, or I feel that you are. It is essential that you understand why Devlin hates us all so much.' She reached for her scissors. 'He was born at a time when, frankly, I think my poor sister had given up all hope of having a child. She and Carey were so delighted with him that he became quite spoiled, but who could blame them? Yet even then the damage was being done. Because Carey and my husband were partners in Archangel, Devlin was led to believe, quite wrongly, that he would have equal rights of inheritance. When—eventually—it was pointed out to him that this could not be so and that Theo would be the heir, he could not accept it. Neither, I fear, could his parents. They began to spend more and more of their time away from here—travelling, sailing. The rift between us grieved my husband terribly. He had grown to rely on Carey and on Devlin too. Theo was only a child, of course.' She picked up another skein of silk and began to thread her needle.

'It was during one of these sailing trips that a squall blew up and Madeleine and Carey lost their lives,' she went on after a small pause. 'Devlin behaved like a madman. He accused us of having driven them away—almost of having caused their deaths.' She shuddered and closed her eyes for a moment. 'Added to our own grief, his attitude was almost more than we could bear. Hard words were spoken—on both sides. Two years later my husband became very ill and sent for Devlin. I hoped with all my heart that the breach between us might be healed, but he made it clear then and later at the funeral that nothing had changed. By that time, of course, he had begun to work actively against us.'

'In what way?' Christina was bewildered by what she had been told.

Mrs Brandon shrugged. 'Devlin, while away at university, had become—imbued with some strange sentiments. When he returned, he behaved as if the *status quo* would no longer suit him. He criticised the running of the plantation—the fact that we produced only sugar. He claimed that the economic difficulties of the West Indies were caused by this form of monoculture—that only the large islands like Barbados should devote themselves to sugar cultivation, and the others should turn instead to agriculture and food production to cut down on costly imports.' She gave a harsh laugh. 'He really seemed to think that his uncle and I would fall in with these views and calmly hand over our land and our livelihood—the plantation which has belonged to the Brandons for generations. He soon discovered his mistake, but he managed to gather round himself a group of people who share his views. They now operate as the "Island Committee".' She folded her embroidery and put it to one side.

'I tell you all this, *mon enfant*, so that you are warned. You are a stranger here and Devlin will not hesitate to use you if he can. His—disappointments have made him bitter. Also——' she paused delicately, 'he is no respecter of innocence. You would do well to avoid him. It will not be difficult—his visits here are few.'

Christina nodded silently. It was not difficult advice to

accept, she thought. The less she saw of Devlin Brandon, the better for her own peace of mind. She was thankful that Mrs Brandon did not know the real reason for her apparent docility. That would be too humiliating!

She spent the next half hour or so taking dictation as Mrs Brandon dealt with her correspondence. There was not a great deal to do, and much of that was trivial, she discovered—responses to fund-raising appeals, social invitations and the like. Mrs Brandon did not lead a sufficiently active life to need a social secretary, Christina thought. It occurred to her that it might be difficult to find sufficient work to keep her occupied, and she resolved that if this situation arose, she would go back to England—or look for another job where she could at least justify her existence.

She typed the few letters there were on a small portable typewriter which had been set on a table in the library downstairs for her. When they were done, she was presumably free again, as Mrs Brandon had given her no further instructions. She debated whether to take them upstairs immediately for signature or wait until she was sent for. She went into the hall and stood looking around her rather irresolutely. Mrs Brandon had said she considered her 'one of the family', but Christina thought she had never felt so utterly isolated in her life. She tried to tell herself robustly that she was feeling disturbed because of what had transpired earlier that morning and the warning from Mrs Brandon which had followed it.

Mrs Brandon had assumed, she thought wryly, that she would be totally in sympathy with what she had said. Yet at school, Christina had heard that the concentration on a single sugar crop was a major reason for the economic ills of the West Indies, and that the production of sugar cane had to be heavily subsidised by the major economic powers. No one could expect such theories to be popular with the plantation owners, many of whom had grown very rich through sugar, and Devlin had probably been less than tactful in putting them forward. But that did not mean he was as much in the wrong as Mrs Brandon had suggested.

She recalled her thoughts with a start, realising that she was under scrutiny. Madame Christophe was passing through the hall carrying a bowl of flowers. As she passed Christina, she gave her a slight nod, but her face remained impassive.

Christina detained her. 'Do you know if Mrs Brandon will want me again this morning?' she asked. 'I've finished her letters and . . .'

Madame Christophe shook her head. 'Her masseuse from Fort Victoire is with her now,' she said. 'Then she will rest until lunchtime. Do you wish me to inform her that you have gone out?'

'Oh, no.' Christina was a little taken aback. 'It's just that I'm not—altogether sure what is expected of me.'

'Are you not, *mademoiselle*?' There was more than a trace of irony in Madame's voice. 'I am sure all will be made clear to you in time. But for now—do you wish to go out? Fort Victoire is quite an interesting town. Louis will bring the car round, if you wish . . .'

'No—please.' Christina felt that odd sense of bewilderment again. It seemed her role of the honoured guest had been reverted to without her being aware of it. 'I think I'll have a look round the garden. I used to do a lot of gardening at home. I expect it will all be very different.' She stopped uncomfortably, aware that she was babbling inanities, but there was something overpowering about Madame Christophe that had a disastrous effect on her precarious poise.

'Yes,' Madame said calmly. 'I daresay everything will be very—different. But Mademoiselle will no doubt accustom herself in time—if she stays.'

Christina watched her go, aware that her heart was beating uncomfortably. There had been nothing to complain of in Madame's manner—she had been quietly polite, respectful even—and yet ... Christina told herself she was being over-imaginative. There must be something in the air of the islands, she thought ruefully, something that made one over-sensitive—too susceptible to impressions. After all, there was very little to disturb her if she tried to be logical about it. She was staying in a beautiful, luxurious home with people who seemed intent on making her feel at ease. Surely she could accept that at its face value, and not try to go delving underneath searching for motives that might not even exist.

It was Devlin Brandon she had to thank for this, she told herself defensively. He was the root cause of all her uneasiness—her uncertainties. She had never hated anyone in her life, but she might—she just might begin with him. He seemed to have the power to spoil everything—the serpent in this Eden. She glanced across at the huge statue—the Archangel trampling the devil under his feet—and bit her lip. That was just a story—a legend. The devil she had to cope with was all too human flesh and blood. She folded her arms across her body in an instinctive gesture of protection, trying vainly to shut out of her memory the sensation of being in his arms, knowing their strength, feeling the lean muscularity of his body against hers.

And he'd known—that was the real humiliation—he'd known quite well precisely what response he could evoke, apparently at will.

But never again, she whispered to herself fiercely. Never again would he have the satisfaction of exploring her vulnerability. There was a kind of bleak triumph in coming to this decision, but she did not dare ask herself, long hours afterwards when the triumph had faded, why only the bleakness remained.

# CHAPTER FIVE

THE week that followed soon adopted a pattern of its own. Christina breakfasted in her room, then went for a walk until Mrs Brandon sent for her. But she restricted her activities to the grounds, and kept away from the beach, much as it grieved her to do so.

Devlin did not come to the house, nor was he mentioned by any of the occupants. Mrs Brandon did not venture any further confidences about the family history, and Christina wondered whether she might not be regretting saying as much as she had done. She did not initiate any inquiries herself, even though there were things she would liked to have known. It had not occurred to her until much later that Mrs Brandon had never mentioned her own child —Theo's father. It was a gap in the story that had not struck her at the time—probably because she had allowed herself to become far too interested in what Mrs Brandon had to say about Devlin, she thought in self-accusation. But now she wondered at the omission.

In her explorations of the house, she had encountered the majority of the past Brandons in portrait form, including a charming study of Mrs Brandon and her sister Madeleine.

Madeleine Brandon looked very much the younger of the two, Christina thought as she studied the painting. There was a gentleness and a humour in her face that her sister had probably never possessed. Even in the pose the artist had demanded, Mrs Brandon looked more rigid, as if she was intent on disciplining herself all the time. But they had both been beautiful, Christina had to acknowledge. There was little wonder that they should both have captured the hearts of the Brandon brothers.

But nowhere could she find any pictorial reference to a child of Charles and Marcelle Brandon—not even among the many photographs that adorned Mrs Brandon's sitting room in their shining silver frames, although there were plenty of pictures of Theo at various stages of his development.

She was curious, but she decided she would simply have to restrain her curiosity. There had been one tragedy in the recent past with the drowning of Carey and Madeleine. Perhaps there had been another, too painful even to mention, and Christina was determined not to re-open old wounds when this could easily be avoided. If Madame Christophe—or Eulalie—had been more easily approachable, she could have asked them, but they were both as distant as ever and she guessed that any attempt on her part to indulge in gossip about the Brandon family would be repudiated.

Somewhat reluctantly, she found she was inevitably seeing a great deal of Theo. As soon as it was obvious his grandmother was prepared to encourage the association, his invitations had come thick and fast. Christina had managed to parry the more energetic of these—including suggestions that they should go riding, and surfing at a beach on the other side of the island—on the grounds that her ankle was still giving her trouble. But this excuse could not prevent him from joining her when she walked in the garden after dinner, although to her relief he made no attempt to carry their relationship beyond a little lighthearted flirting.

She found too that when she sunbathed by the swimming pool in the afternoon while Mrs Brandon rested indoors, Theo was often there. This surprised her, as she imagined his plantation duties would keep him fully occupied during the day. He certainly complained enough about them, and about the alleged shortcomings of Clive Maynard, the plantation manager, who lived with his wife and two children in a small bungalow on the opposite side of the Archangel estate.

Christina had met the Maynards when Theo took her on a tour of the plantation one day. She had been fascinated by everything she had seen, asking eager questions but aware at the same time that Theo's interest did not match her own. He answered most of her inquiries but without enthusiasm, and eventually referred her to Clive, whom they encountered at the crushing plant, and who insisted they should accompany him back to his bungalow for lunch. Christina had liked Lorna Maynard, and had thoroughly enjoyed the chicken and rice dish that she had served with long cool drinks in frosted glasses, but she had been embarrassed at the same time by Theo's obvious boredom with the whole thing and was relieved when Clive announced that he had to go back to work and the impromptu party broke up.

Theo had been surprised and a little put out when she tackled him about his attitude as they drove away in the Range Rover.

'Clive's an adequate manager and he gets well paid. I don't have to make him a bosom friend of him as well,' he said coldly.

Christina stared at him. 'But I'm an employee too and you don't treat me like that,' she pointed out.

Theo smiled, forgetting his annoyance and exerting all his considerable charm. 'You come into a very different category, sweetie,' he told her.

Christina subsided with a vague feeling of dissatisfaction. She hoped that Lorna had not been upset by Theo's desultory replies and barely concealed yawns during lunch. She was too pleasant for that. She wondered too if Theo had been peeved because Clive knew so much more about the production of sugar than he did, and was so much more willing to talk about it. It seemed to her that Theo's basic interest in the plantation was more proprietorial than in-

dustrious. He enjoyed the respect paid to him as the future
owner, but did not want to become deeply involved in its
workings. It occurred to her, not for the first time, that if
Mrs Brandon was not the easiest person in the world to
work for, then her grandson would probably come a close
second.

It gave her almost a feeling of pleasure to turn down his
invitation to go out to dinner that night on the specious
grounds that she had letters to write. Afterwards, she justified herself by actually writing to Mr Frith. It was longer
than she had originally intended because she decided it
might be politic to remain upstairs for most of the evening.
She described the house, and told the story of how it
acquired its name, and she related what family history she
knew. She made it as lighthearted and amusing as she could,
stressing the enjoyable side of life on Ste Victoire. Reading
it through before she sealed the envelope, she thought it
would allay any lingering worries Mrs Frith might still be
entertaining about her well-being.

But Theo regarded her refusal of his invitation as merely
a temporary setback, and he made sure that the next time
he asked her his grandmother was present. Uncomfortably
aware of Mrs Brandon's approving smile, Christina knew
she could hardly refuse again. Besides, this time she had no
excuse, either real or feigned, so she reluctantly accepted.

She still hadn't fully worked out the reasons behind her
reluctance as she changed that evening. She had decided to
wear her nearest approximation to an evening dress—very
simple in white silky crepe, the skirt flaring slightly to mid-
calf length. The clinging bodice was held up by narrow
shoulder straps, but a long matching scarf acted as a cover-
up. She had piled her hair up on top of her head in a loose
knot. A touch of mascara on her long lashes, and some gloss
for her mouth, and she was ready.

As she descended the stairs, she was glad she had made
the effort as Theo was waiting for her in the hall, resplen-

dent in a white dinner jacket. She had to admit that the
formal attire set off his dark good looks perfectly and gave
him a look of added maturity.

He came forward to the foot of the stairs and took her
hand.

'You look enchanting, Tina.' He bent and pressed his
lips to her palm. It gave her an odd sensation—not unpleasant, but not wholly enjoyable either, and she removed
her hand from his grasp very firmly, her colour heightened.
Just as she did so, she became aware that Mrs Brandon
had appeared in the doorway of the salon and was watching
them. Christina could not tell whether she had witnessed
Theo's caress and its aftermath. Her expression was enigmatic, but she did not look displeased. She wished them
both an enjoyable evening, and adjured Theo to drive carefully and not keep Christina out too late before she turned
away.

'We'll have dinner at the Hotel Montfort,' Theo said as
he opened the passenger door for Christina. Not the Range
Rover tonight, she noticed, but a low-slung elegant sports
car which looked as if it could pack a powerful punch
under that sleek bonnet. 'The food's good, but it's not
exactly a hot spot, so I thought we could go on afterwards to
the Beguine. That's the club I mentioned.'

'It sounds fine.' Christina leaned back on the luxuriously
padded seat. Now that she was here, she was determined to
enjoy herself. 'Isn't the Beguine also a dance?'

'Oh, yes.' Theo slanted her a grin as he switched on the
ignition. 'We only have a watered-down version here,
though. If you want to see it danced properly you have to
see it on Martinique. I suppose you didn't ... No, Grand'-
mère would definitely not have approved!'

With her memories of the roads, Christina had not been
looking forward to the drive to Fort Victoire, but it was not
as bad as she had anticipated. Perhaps being in an open car
had something to do with it, she thought, because there

was no actual improvement in the road itself. It was narrow and twisted and turned along the top of the cliff. Glancing down, Christina caught a disturbing glimpse of a near precipitous drop to the sea below, with only a flimsy guard rail to protect the unwary. She swallowed and fixed her gaze firmly in front of her, hoping devoutly that Theo knew the road as well as he appeared to know the car. She had to admit to herself that the speed they were maintaining was quite sedate under the circumstances. She was surprised as she had not suspected Theo capable of so much consideration.

Nevertheless she was quite glad when she saw the patch of lights in the distance that announced they were approaching Fort Victoire.

'Our tourist trap,' Theo said lightly.

She glanced sideways at him. 'I thought tourists weren't encouraged.'

'By us they're not, but there are other interests now, and they're making sure they're heard,' Theo said a little peevishly. 'Bellairs who owns the Montfort is one of them—and my dear cousin Dev is another, of course.'

Her mouth felt suddenly dry. 'Of course.'

Theo's lips were thin. 'They have all kinds of little schemes—a marina for boats, no less, and several more hotels—a country club. I daresay it would all have been a *fait accompli* by now—if they could have got the land.'

'Is there none available?'

His smile was small and triumphant. 'Not while there are Brandons at Archangel, Tina. We still own most of the land—and the whip hand as well.'

Christina moistened her lips. 'I—I see.'

She thought she did, too. It was something she had never experienced before—this enjoyment of power for its own sake. She found it alarming.

She was conscious of it again while they were dining. The food and service were impeccable, but she found the

air of deference with which they were treated almost overwhelming. And Theo, she thought, biting her lip, was in his
element—sending a message to the chef, arguing over
various vintages with the wine waiter as if he was a noted
connoisseur of many years' standing instead of a boy barely
out of his teens. She knew that people were watching them,
and her embarrassment grew.

She began to wonder if she could feign a headache once
the meal was over. She found she did not want to have to
spend the remainder of the evening watching Theo lord it
over Fort Victoire.

But as she began her excuses, Theo became mutinous. It
had been stuffy in the dining room, he would grant her that,
but she couldn't break the evening up so quickly. They
would walk to the Beguine, and the fresh air would clear
her head. He was so insistent that Christina felt she could
not persist in her objections. Her position was a difficult
one. She was here after all with her employer's full appro-
bation, but Mrs Brandon might not be too pleased if she
cut the evening short with some lame excuse. Theo was
evidently her pride and joy and was spoiled as a result.
Watching him act the part of Mr Brandon of Archangel
might have to be one of her duties, and she would have to
regard it in that light.

In spite of the Brandons' opposition, tourists had begun
to discover Ste Victoire, she thought, as they entered the
Beguine. Nearly all the tables, set on a raised gallery running round the dance floor, were occupied and the floor
itself was crowded.

She turned to Theo. 'There doesn't seem to be much
room . . .

He ignored her, summoning a waiter with a snap of his
fingers. As if by magic a table for two appeared at the edge
of the floor. By the time they reached it, candles had been
lit on it and a flower arrangement had been placed in its
centre.

Christina sat down in the chair that was being held for her. 'I'm beginning to know how Royalty must feel,' she said. It was intended to be tart, but Theo obviously regarded the remark as a compliment to his stage management and merely smiled at her.

'You'll get used to it,' he said casually.

She had to quell an impulse to tell him she had no intention of doing anything of the sort, and hoped she did not look as out of place as she felt. A quick glance around the surrounding tables reassured her somewhat. The clientele were smart, and the jewellery worn by the women also suggested wealth, but her own outfit stood up well to any competition. Drinks were brought in tall frosted glasses —a mixture of fruit juices, pineapple and lime among them, with something pleasantly potent underneath it all.

'Planter's Punch,' Theo told her, lifting his glass towards her. She returned the gesture rather awkwardly, aware of speculative looks from people sitting near them. Theo made a spectacular escort, she realised, encountering some openly envious glances from some of the younger women. She still felt thoroughly self-conscious, but it wasn't quite the unpleasant sensation it had been. She sipped appreciatively at her drink and returned Theo's smile.

'Would you like to dance?'

'Presently,' she said.

It was only a small band, but they had a beguiling rhythm. She found her foot was tapping to it almost in spite of herself. But at the same time she didn't want to dance. She had an appalled vision of a deferential space being cleared for Theo and herself on the small circular floor, having to dance, the cynosure of all eyes from the clustering tables. It would be like being on stage with the spotlight glaring down.

Theo was glancing round him with lifted eyebrows. 'I don't know where all these people come from,' he said in a bored tone, not bothering to lower his voice. 'This place is going to become quite unbearable if the situation continues. And this isn't even the season.'

He was looking beyond her and she saw his gaze sharpen. He gave a muffled exclamation which she hoped she had misheard. His eyes met hers angrily, then he got slowly to his feet with obvious reluctance, and she knew without having to be told who was standing just behind them.

'It's a small world.' Theo tried for a light tone and missed.

'It's a very small island,' said Dev Brandon. A waiter brought a chair and he sat down without being invited. Christina felt her stomach muscles twine themselves into a tight knot of tension. He looked her over and smiled—if that was the way to describe a movement of the lips that held neither amusement nor pleasure.

'A daiquiri, please,' he told the hovering waiter, and then sat back in his chair with the air of a man with the whole evening in front of him. Theo was furious and not bothering to hide it, Christina noticed. She felt as if she had just woken from a nightmare only to find it was actually happening.

Theo reseated himself sullenly. 'I didn't expect to see you here this evening.'

'Naturally,' Dev returned blandly. 'But I do like to keep an eye on my investments.'

'So it is true.' Theo sent him a concentrated glare. 'Grand'mère heard that you'd gone in with Frampton and Bellairs, but she didn't believe it.'

'I'm glad to know she still has faith in me.' Dev's tone was openly satirical. 'Even if it is only a baseless conviction about my total lack of business acumen.'

'If you must know, even Grand'mère didn't think you would be so totally disloyal to the Brandon name,' Theo flung at him recklessly.

Devlin produced a silver case from his pocket and lit a cheroot, watching Theo almost meditatively for a minute.

Then he said quite pleasantly, 'That, my dear Theo, is a subject on which you are hardly qualified to comment.'

There were suddenly undercurrents to the conversation that Christina could only guess at. Summoning all her courage, she intervened, 'Please—people are watching us.'

Dev's eyes flickered carelessly over her. 'Don't let it worry you. We're thinking of advertising the Brandon feud in the brochures next year as an added attraction. It's already part of the scenery as far as the locals are concerned.'

'But I'm not one of them,' she said in a low voice. She glanced up and met his gaze and saw an expression of faint surprise there.

'No,' he said after a moment. 'You're just along for the ride, aren't you, honey girl. But you only have yourself to blame if it gets bumpy.'

'Leave Tina out of this,' Theo broke in aggressively, and Devlin raised his eyebrows.

'Tina?' he queried, then shook his head decisively. 'No, not Tina. Christy rarely, if ever—but never Tina.'

'What are you talking about?' Theo demanded. Devlin grinned sardonically at Christina, and she felt the betraying colour rise in her cheeks.

'A private joke,' he said lightly. 'Don't let it bother you, Theo.' He lifted the glass the waiter had brought him to his lips. Above it, his eyes watched Christina. She looked away hurriedly, disturbed by his scrutiny. It was a good thing she had not been looking forward to this evening, she thought helplessly. Oh, why of all the people in the world had he had to be here?

The waiter returned. 'Telephone, Mr Brandon.'

She began to draw a sigh of relief, but it was short-lived. It was Theo, not Dev, the waiter was addressing. Theo looked up at him incredulously.

'For me? But who . . .?' He bit back an imprecation, then got up, scraping his chair, and followed the waiter.

Christina sat very quiet, hoping against hope that Devlin

would take the hint and go back to his own table or wherever else he had sprung from. It was unnerving to have him sitting so close to her. The table was too small for more than two people. His leg was practically brushing hers. She would have liked to have moved, but she knew he would guess the reason why and make one of his barbed remarks. It was better—more dignified—to sit perfectly still and pretend he did not exist.

'It won't work.' It was as if he could read her thoughts, damn him. 'I'm in the mood to be entertained, Christina, and you're just the person to do it.'

'I have nothing to say to you, Mr Brandon,' she told him coldly. He smiled faintly.

'Then don't try. I didn't ask you to talk. I can find all the entertainment I need by sitting and looking at you. You have a lovely body and that's a very sexy dress.'

'I thought I was under-developed,' she flashed, and could have bitten her tongue out.

He was laughing openly now. 'So that still rankles, does it? All right, I take it back. You have, my dear Miss Bennett, the type of figure that improves on intimate acquaintance. Will that do?'

'No,' she said, loathing him. 'It won't—and you haven't. Any intimate acquaintance, I mean.'

'Well, we can soon rectify that.' He got up, reaching for her wrist and pulling her to her feet. 'Come and dance.'

'I will not.' Bright spots of colour burned in her cheeks.

'It's either that or make a scene,' he said equably. 'And don't plead your ankle as an excuse,' he added, as she hesitated. 'That was better days ago, and you know it.'

Quivering with temper, she allowed herself to be led down the short flight of wooden steps that led to the dance floor. Her body was rigid as he drew her into his arms.

'Relax.' His voice sounded mockingly in her ear. 'I promise not to rape you in front of all these people.'

'You wouldn't get the chance,' she muttered unwisely.

'I've had the chance.' His tone was very quiet, but there was a note in it which made her whole body feel warm. And the dreadful thing was that she could not even deny it. If he had gone on kissing her—touching her that day at the beach house she would have been his for the taking. She knew it—now, but it seemed that he had always known it. She swallowed and stared icily at the lapel of his jacket.

'And it is a sexy dress,' he went on in the same quiet voice. 'White and silken. It's hard to know where the dress ends and your skin begins.'

Something seemed to be constricting her breathing. When she had got it under control, she said, 'Please—don't say things like that. I know you're only trying to embarrass me. Will you take my word for it that you've succeeded and leave it at that?'

'You credit me with some strange ambitions,' he said in an odd tone. 'However, if you want to call a truce, I'm perfectly willing. We'll talk about something else. When is your engagement to Theo going to be announced?'

She was so startled that she forgot to move her feet and nearly fell.

'What are you talking about?' she demanded breathlessly.

'Isn't English your native tongue? I'm sorry.'

She could have screamed at him, but she held on to her patience.

'What are you insinuating—about Theo and me?'

'Nothing at all,' he said coolly. 'That is why you've come here, isn't it?'

The rhythm of the music changed. The beat quickened slightly. She was no longer in his arms. They were slightly apart, and she was moving mechanically to the music, its soft insistent beat seeming the only reality in a world that had changed to quicksand around her.

'Well, isn't it?' His tone had hardened, demanding a reply.

She drew a long quivering breath. 'No. I've told you

why I came. Why won't you believe me? I—I didn't even know Theo existed until I met him—that first day. Of course I'm not engaged to him. I hardly know him!'

'I wasn't suggesting it was a love match.' The silver eyes were steel hard as they looked down into hers.

'Then what ...?' she relapsed almost helplessly into silence.

'You told me yourself you were penniless,' he said softly. 'Maybe, in your circumstances, marriage wouldn't be too high a price to pay to become Mrs Brandon of Archangel.'

She felt her hands curl into fists at her sides. Behind the smiling mask, she was cold and dead inside. When she spoke, she was amazed by the normality of her own voice.

'You think, then, that I'm for sale?' It was quite amazing how much it cost her to ask that. Yet why should she care what he thought of her? Of all the opinions in the world, his should be her least concern. So why then this hurt, like a knife twisting deep inside her?

He gave a slight shrug, his mouth twisting cynically. 'It's what my aunt thinks that matters, and I hardly think she would have brought you here if she didn't consider the bargain was made.'

'You're quite wrong.' She moistened her lips with the tip of her tongue. 'But I suppose I can't altogether blame you for misjudging me. Your aunt said that your—disappointments over the inheritance had made you bitter. I don't suppose even she guesses how right she is. I can quite understand why you don't want Theo to marry, of course. What I can't understand is why you should think I'm part of some weird conspiracy to deprive you of Archangel.'

'Oh, I acquit you of that,' he said. 'That "weird conspiracy", as you so aptly put it, began many years ago— before my aunt probably even knew you existed. But it alters nothing. If you genuinely mean what you say, then you'll get out of here and back to England as soon as you can.'

The drumming rose to a crescendo and stopped. Around them laughing couples were dispersing from the floor and walking back to their tables. Christina turned too, very conscious of his hand on her arm.

'I've already told you that's quite impossible,' she said, her voice shaking slightly. 'Now will you please let go of me—and leave me alone.'

'You mean—leave you to Theo,' he said, and there was a note underlying his tone that made her shiver in spite of the heat of the room. She lifted her chin defiantly.

'If that's what you want to think—yes,' she said. She wrenched her arm free of his grasp with a strength she had not known she possessed, and walked with unsteady legs up the steps and back to the table.

She felt almost sick with nerves. What a fiasco this evening she had not even wanted had become! She had left behind her an angry man, and she had little doubt that another even angrier was waiting for her.

But here it seemed she was mistaken. When she got back to the table, Theo was waiting, smiling and relaxed.

'You dance well,' he complimented her lightly. 'It was almost a greater pleasure to sit here and watch you than join the hurly-burly myself.' He paused and gave her a long, considering look. 'Are you quite well, Tina? You look pale.'

She seized on his words with relief. 'Actually, I have a headache. I think it's the punch. I'm not really used to alcohol, you see.'

'Naturally not. One forgets how potent our drinks can be to someone who has not yet acquired a head for them. I'll take you home. It is time we were making a move anyway, or Grand'mère will be worrying about us.'

Christina felt confused as he ushered her solicitously to the door. She had expected some sort of tantrum. He had been certainly spoiling for one before he had been called away to the telephone. Perhaps he'd had time to think calmly and reason out that Devlin was only trying to needle

him. It was an encouraging thought as it implied a level of
maturity in Theo she had not detected before.

She was very silent in the car as they drove towards Archangel, and knew that her companion was giving her curious
looks. Carrying on the pretence of a headache, she leaned
back against the seat, closing her eyes and allowing her
thoughts to run riot.

In spite of her defence of herself, she had been shaken to
the core by what Devlin Brandon had said. Yet in many
ways she knew she should not have been surprised. He had
made it clear in Martinique that he thought she was on the
make in some way, and his present suspicions were simply
an extension of that earlier belief. Nothing she could say or
do could apparently justify her presence on Ste Victoire,
she thought, and she was a fool to continue to try.

It was wretched to discover too how deeply his jealousy
and disappointment over Theo had flawed his personality.
He was an overwhelmingly attractive man, she had to acknowledge that, but his attitude to his aunt was practically
paranoid. She tried vainly to stifle the regrets that this
realisation inevitably roused in her.

It was madness even to give him a second thought, she
told herself robustly. Devlin Brandon was a taker—and she
did not want to be taken. It was useless to think that he
might have any genuine feelings or emotions. His treatment
of her had made it clear that he regarded women as play-
things, to be used for an hour or two, then discarded. He
had probably known what he had aroused in her and been
amused by it. Well, he would never get the chance again,
nor would she allow him to make mischief between her employer and herself by his snide allegations. He was an
angry and a bitter man, but she could not allow herself to
be affected by that anger and bitterness. His quarrels with
Mrs Brandon were of no concern to her.

She felt exhausted when the car finally drew up, as if
she had been arguing with herself rather than reiterating

some known truths. All she wanted to do was escape upstairs to solitude, but that was denied her.

Theo was urging her towards the salon. They would have some coffee, he directed imperiously, and Madame Christophe would bring her a painkiller for her headache. Christina gave way reluctantly, after a half-hearted protest. She did not want a further *tête-à-tête* with Theo that night, and she was conscious of a feeling of relief when she saw that Mrs Brandon was still up, sitting waiting for them with the inevitable embroidery in her lap.

Theo sat down beside her, kissed her hands and launched himself into a recital of the evening's events that bore little relation to Christina's own memories of it. For one thing, he mentioned a long list of people who had been at the hotel and afterwards at the Beguine in a way that suggested that she and Theo had been members of a large group instead of studiously on their own. The one name he did not speak was Devlin's, and Christina gathered with growing amazement that that particular part of the evening was to be regarded as not having happened.

The arrival of Madame Christophe with the coffee tray was Mrs Brandon's signal to depart. She rose slowly and painfully from the sofa and made her way to the door, after kissing Theo affectionately and bestowing a slightly more punctilious goodnight on Christina.

As soon as the door had closed behind her and they were alone, Christina turned to Theo, openly indignant. 'Why didn't you tell her the truth?'

'Because that was not what she would have wanted to hear.' Theo lifted his shoulders in a gesture of insouciance. 'What harm has been done? You must not be so scrupulous, Tina. When you have been with us longer, you will discover the best way to handle Grand'mère.'

Christina bit back the instinctive retort that boiled up in her. She picked up the small medicine cup from the tray, and swallowed the tablet it contained with a mouthful of coffee. Theo leaned back against the sofa and watched her through half-closed eyes.

'She was very happy tonight,' he went on after a pause. 'I could see she thought we made a handsome couple. It is charming that you should be fair while I am dark. We look good together, Tina, don't you think?'

Christina set the cup back on the tray, her hand trembling a little. Theo seemed to be building up to a flirtation —the one thing she had wanted to avoid.

'I don't think I've ever been invited out on aesthetic grounds before,' she commented, keeping her voice light. 'I'm sure you're quite aware of your own good looks, Theo. You don't need any reassurance from me.'

He replaced his own cup on the tray and moved closer to her. She tried to edge away imperceptibly, but his hand shot out and gripped the fold of her skirt.

'Not reassurance, maybe, but I have other needs, Tina. I need love—a woman's affection.'

She sat very still, her mind working furiously. She tried to smile. 'Well, I'll be fond of you, Theo, if you'd let me go to bed. I'm worn out.'

'That is unfortunate,' he said, and there was a snap in his voice. 'But I am not ready to go to bed yet. Don't play hard to get with me, Tina.'

She gasped with indignation. 'Of all the damned cheek——' she began, and glanced down, startled. His hand was moving the fold of silk, pushing it away from her knee up towards her thigh. 'And you can stop that now!' She slapped him hard.

'You say that—you do that to me.' His voice was harsh, his face set and suddenly ugly. 'But *ce brave* Devlin—he is another matter, *non*? Do you not think I saw the way you looked at him? The way you moved your body inside your dress while you were dancing for him.' He lunged at her, pinning her against the sofa back. His mouth sought hers greedily, and she tried vainly to turn her head away to escape his wet, seeking lips. His hands were on her breasts, squeezing them so that she gasped in pain, then his fingers were pulling at her skirt again. For a moment she lay still, too horrified by this sudden display of passion to resist. Then summoning all her strength, she pushed at him wildly, violently. He was off balance, half kneeling over her, and her move sent him sprawling on to the floor. For a moment he lay there glaring at her, then suddenly he turned over on to his stomach and began to cry. Her lips parted in disbelief as she stared down at him, prostrate at her feet, his whole body shaking with sobs.

'Theo, for God's sake.' She felt totally helpless. 'What in the world's come over you? You must stop this—stop crying.'

He raised his head and looked at her. His handsome face was blotched and swollen with tears. He looked very young.

'How can I not cry, when you are so cruel to me?' he demanded.

'Don't talk such nonsense,' she said angrily. 'Did you really think that I was going to let you ...' she paused, searching for the right words. She couldn't say 'make love'. To use those words in respect of that brutal, selfish assault would be a desecration. 'Let you—use me in return for a night out?'

'No, no.' He got up on to his knees. 'You don't understand. I lost control of myself and I regret that—I can't tell you how much. But if I did, Tina, don't blame me too much. It's only because I love you ...'

'Stop it!' she jumped to her feet, her face white. 'I'm not going to let you talk like that. It's ridiculous!'

'Just now you were angry because I did not speak the truth. Now you are angry because I do. Tina, forgive me. I did not mean to tell you yet, but when I saw you with Devlin tonight, when I knew how he schemed to get you away from me, I was so jealous.'

'You've no right to be jealous—and no reason either.'

This was a bad dream, and soon, soon, please God, she would wake from it.

'No?' He rose to his feet and faced her. 'When I got to the telephone my caller had conveniently rung off, and when I returned you had gone—with him. At once it was clear. That call was just a ruse to get me away from the table—one of his friends playing a trick. Always he has envied me—envied me this plantation—because Grand'-mère preferred me. And now he envies me my woman.'

'Let us get one thing quite clear,' Christina said very steadily. 'I am not your woman.'

There was a long electric pause, then Theo turned away, thrusting his hands petulantly into his trousers pockets.

'You are saying that to hurt me,' he flung at her over his shoulder.

'No, Theo, it's the truth.' She made herself speak gently. With a kind of detached anguish, she realised that one of the straps on her dress was broken, and she lifted a fold of the bodice to cover her breast. Someone had said—a long time ago—that it was hard to tell where the dress ended and her skin began. She felt a sob rising in her throat, and bit it back. 'If I've ever given you cause to think anything else, I'm sorry. I—I realise in the circumstances it was a mistake to go out with you this evening, but it won't happen again. Goodnight.'

As she walked to the door, she knew a moment's fear that he would come after her, but he made no attempt to move. She closed the door and stood for a moment leaning against it, trying to regain her calm. Then she made herself walk without hurrying up the stairs to her room.

She was thankful there was no one around to see her. One glance in her mirror told the whole story. As well as her torn dress, some of her hair had become loosened from its knot during the struggle and was hanging untidily around her ears, and her lip gloss was smudged. She felt dirty all over, and she shuddered.

Shedding her clothes, she walked into the bathroom and ran hot water into the tub. As she scrubbed and rinsed her skin, she began almost insensibly to feel better, but she knew at the same time that her feelings were the least of her problems. She was faced with the unpalatable fact that Dev Brandon seemed to be right, after all.

She was sure that nothing she had said or done could have led Theo to think that ne had some claim on her. Therefore his belief must have been prompted by some outside agency, and Mrs Brandon was the obvious—indeed, the only choice. Christina had always felt disturbed by her employer's willing acceptance of her grandson's interest in her. She was not of their world, and she had no money, and she was not so naïve as to believe these things did not matter. There was no way in which she could be considered a suitable bride for the heir to Archangel, unless they had fallen deeply and passionately in love with each other.

Did Theo love her? She got out of the bath and began to dry herself on one of the big towelling bath sheets provided for the purpose. She tried to consider the matter objectively. He admired her, and had made no secret of it— but love? There had been few signs of that. There had been no tenderness, no desire to seek a corresponding arousal in his behaviour downstairs. For one brief heart-thudding instant, she recalled another mouth on hers, other hands touching her in intimate exploration, then she determinedly put that memory away from her too. That had nothing to do with love either—just an arrogant wish to add her name to his apparently endless list of conquests. She could only be thankful she had come to her senses before being carried away on that sweet golden tide of wantonness. At the same time, some inner demon muttered that if she had succumbed to Devlin, at least her present predicament would not exist. Maybe that was what he had intended all along, and his lovemaking had been prompted less by desire for her than a wish to make mischief as Theo had suggested.

With a groan, she dropped the bath sheet in a damp crumpled heap and walked through into the bedroom. She stood for a moment, taking a long hard look at herself in the mirror. She was slim—indeed, if one was being critical, skinny might even be the word—or underdeveloped, she thought, biting her lip. Her breasts were small, and the curve of her hips gently rounded rather than voluptuous. She gazed for a few seconds more before turning away and reaching for her gingham nightgown. Nothing there, she thought, to drive any man wild with desire, as she would do well to remind herself.

Devlin Brandon's motives seemed clear enough, she decided, stifling the instinctive pain that brought in its train. What had Mrs Brandon said? 'No respecter of innocence'. It was shaming to think that she had almost been prepared to sacrifice that innocence to gratify a man with little but malice on his mind.

But Theo's motivation was more difficult to conjecture. It was not the pass he had made—she supposed rather wearily she might have seen that coming—but the avowal of love and the expectation of some sort of prolonged relationship that had followed it were its most disturbing features.

Only one thing seemed certain—she would have to get away, and fast. So first thing tomorrow, she would see Mrs Brandon and hand in her notice. She sighed. There seemed nothing for it but to write to Mr Frith, explaining her situation and begging a temporary loan to enable her to get back to England. She was sure he would help her even though he would be surprised to get an appeal for help so close on the heels of her other communication which had been couched in thoroughly optimistic terms. Once she was back in England, she would have to take whatever work was going and pay him back somehow. It was a frankly depressing prospect, especially when she had thought she had left those sort of worries behind her.

She put a hand to her head. The fictitious headache had become a factual one, and bed seemed suddenly very inviting, although she did not expect to get much sleep. The sheets as she crept between them felt cool to the heat of her body, and the softness of the pillow cradled her like the shoulder of a friend.

And I need a friend, was her last drowsy thought as sleep, aided by the tablet she had taken downstairs, claimed her.

# CHAPTER SIX

As soon as she was dressed the following morning, Christina went along to Mrs Brandon's rooms. She knocked at the outer door of the suite, and after a short pause the door was opened by Eulalie, who gave her a sullen look.

'Madame is not ready for you yet,' she said, and made to close the door again, but Christina forestalled her.

'Please ask her to see me,' she said, determinedly walking past Eulalie into the sitting room.

Eulalie hesitated for a moment, then walked with a flounce back into the bedroom beyond and closed the door. Christina wandered over to the window and stood gazing out, absorbing the beauty of the gardens and the blue gleam of the sea in the distance. In many ways, it would be hard to leave, she thought, just as she was beginning to come to terms with these exotic but alien surroundings. She thought of the silver-sanded beach, and the palm trees that fringed it, and the warmth of the rippling water. These were things she would never be able to forget, she knew, but there would be other less safe memories that she would have to take with her too, and her stomach contracted painfully as a sudden image of Devlin Brandon rose in her mind with his cool eyes and that casual, careless grace of movement. Do what she might when she was gone from this place, she would carry him with her. He was part of it all—of this house, the beach, Fort Victoire—even Martinique.

She gave a deep sigh, and turned to give an impatient glance at the closed bedroom door. Mrs Brandon was in no hurry to accede to her request. Perhaps last night's happenings had been brought to her ears, and she was showing her displeasure. Perhaps Christina would not have to give her notice in after all. Maybe her employer was waiting to sack her. She gave a wry smile. Somehow she did not think so. The more she thought about it, the more evident it seemed that Mrs Brandon was deliberately encouraging an intimate relationship between her grandson and a little nobody from England. The only thing remaining in doubt was why she should be doing this, but Christina had already decided she did not really want to know. All she wanted was out. And if she was honest, it was not simply Theo and his unwanted attentions she needed to escape from, but the ambivalence of her feelings about Devlin Brandon—the enemy she had so nearly allowed to become her lover. She was shocked by the intensity of the emotions he could arouse in her. She could only be thankful that he would never know, and that her self-betrayal had only been brief.

The bedroom door opened and Eulalie appeared in the doorway, indicating with a brief succinct jerk of her head that Christina's presence was required at last. Christina braced herself mentally and then walked into the room with an outward tranquility she was far from feeling.

Mrs Brandon was sitting up in bed, wrapped in a silk bedjacket in an attractive cyclamen shade. Her breakfast tray had been set to one side and she was engaged in looking through the morning's mail. She glanced up as Christina entered with slightly raised brows, but her attitude was not unwelcoming.

'Good morning, *ma chère*. This is an early visit. Has some problem arisen?'

Well, it was the opening she had wanted, Christina thought ruefully. She gave a little nod.

'Sit down.' Mrs Brandon gestured towards a fragile gilt chair, indicating that Christina should pull it up to the bed. She complied with a sinking heart. This interview would have been far easier if Mrs Brandon had been downright hostile or even in one of her regal moods. This morning

she seemed to have reverted to the old friend of Aunt
Grace who had been so persuasive back in England. 'Now,'
she leaned forward and patted Christina's unresponsive
hand. 'What is the trouble? Surely not that little *contre-
temps* with Theo last night?'

Christina flushed and withdrew her hand. 'Then you
know about that?'

'*Naturellement*. There is little that happens on Archangel that I am not acquainted with,' Mrs Brandon returned composedly.

'Then it won't come as any surprise to you when I say—
I have to give you my notice, *madame*, and leave here.'

Mrs Brandon leaned back against her pillows. Her smile
faded into an almost tangible chill. 'Why so?'

'Surely it's obvious.' Christina gripped her hand together
in her lap. 'I simply can't stay here in this house after what
has happened.'

'And why not? Because a silly boy allowed his ardour to
get the better of him and lost his head momentarily? Has
that never happened to you before, Christina? I am amazed
if so. The young men in England must be extremely cold-
blooded.'

Christina bent her head. 'It's very easy to dismiss me as
being a naïve child, *madame*,' she said in a low voice. 'But
you were not there. You don't know what happened.'

'I know enough. Theo came to confess to me at once.'
Mrs Brandon examined the ruby and diamond ring on her
right hand with minute care. 'I understand there was
some damage to your dress—such a shame, it was so charming—for which he is anxious to make amends. I do not
recommend any of the island shops, but he would be happy
to escort you to Martinique to select a new dress and . . .'

'Mrs Brandon, you seem determined to ignore what I've
said. I have asked you to accept my notice.'

'Oh, no, Christina.' Mrs Brandon gave a decisive shake
of her immaculately coiffed head. 'I am not prepared to do

that, *mon enfant*. You are an attractive girl and I think you have not yet come to terms with that. Theo's attentions were—premature, I agree, but . . .'

'The word "premature" suggests that they might become acceptable at some future time,' Christina interrupted her again. A feeling of desperation was beginning to assail her. 'I have to tell you, *madame*, that this just isn't so. And please don't hope for anything different.' She broke off, afraid she had said too much.

Mrs Brandon had become very pale and her lips were drawn into a straight line.

'I think,' she said, and her voice was strained, 'I think it would be better, Christina, if we were to pretend that this conversation had never taken place. You may go now. When you are calmer, I will send Theo to you to apologise. You will be good enough to forgive him. I assure you he is finding it very hard to forgive himself.'

'There's no need for that—please.' Christina felt that the last thing she wanted was a probably emotional scene with Theo abasing himself. 'If you would just accept my notice and allow me to leave at the end of the month.'

'But what I am attempting to convey to you, Christina, is that that will not be possible. I do not wish you to leave.' Mrs Brandon's agitation was increasing perceptibly. 'You have become—necessary to me.'

'To you, *madame*, or to your plans for the future?' Christina demanded, and saw the older woman start. There was a silence and when Mrs Brandon spoke again, her tone was quieter, almost placatory.

'You must forgive me, Christina. As we become older, we do not also necessarily grow wiser. I made the grave mistaking that because I harboured a wish very dear to my heart and that of your godmother, you would in time wish for it too. I see now that is not so, and I ask your pardon.'

Christina stared at her. She felt totally confused at this

unexpected humbling of herself by her employer. And what had she said?

'You spoke of Aunt Grace . . .' she began tentatively, and Mrs Brandon nodded.

'We made a plan while we were at school,' she said, a reminiscent smile playing around her mouth. 'I would have a son, and she would have a daughter, and they would marry. Grace—did not forget, and neither did I. That was why when I saw the notice of her death in a newspaper, I came to fetch you—so that the wish of our youth could be fulfilled.'

Christina sat very still, her body tense. She found it difficult to take in what Mrs Brandon was saying. Was she implying that Aunt Grace had bargained with her about her future? Was that why she had been brought here—so that she could fulfil her side of a bargain she had not even been aware existed? She felt a tight knot of something like desperation begin to curl itself in her midriff. She had to speak, and quickly—to make her position clear.

'I'm sorry,' she said, aware of the shake in her voice, 'but I knew nothing of this, and if I had not known it I would not have come here.' She saw Mrs Brandon stiffen and rushed on. 'I'm sure everyone makes plans like this—for children. But they don't seriously expect that they're going to work out when the children grow up.'

'I expected it.' Mrs Brandon's eyes were very bright. They held Christina's almost magnetically. 'And so did your godmother. Consider, Christina, what else have you to hope for? A brilliant career? It seems hardly likely, does it, with your lack of qualifications. Unless you wish to spend your life as a dependent spinster, marriage seems the best answer—indeed the only answer.'

Christina's heart was thudding. 'Thank you,' she managed, 'for painting such a graphic picture of my prospects.'

Mrs Brandon leaned back against her pillows. 'I am only trying to be realistic,' she pointed out. 'I cannot understand why you should find marriage with my grandson such an alarming prospect. Does the idea of being mistress of Archangel not appeal to you?'

Christina bent her head. There was a struggle going on inside herself that it was imperative Mrs Brandon did not even guess at, or she might be lost. Of course it appealed to her. She would not have been human if she had not fully enjoyed the kind of luxury at her disposal since she had arrived. The house seemed to function on well-oiled machinery, and the service provided was unobtrusive but excellent. At the back of all this was wealth, she knew, the sort of money you heard about but never actually possessed.

Yet at the same time, beating in her brain, she seemed to hear a man's scornful words, *'Is marriage too high a price to pay ... too high a price?'* Eyes like silver ice seemed to flay the skin from her body, and a long controlled shudder went through her. No, she could never marry Theo, not now. Her first lesson on what passion could be between a man and a woman might have been brief, but she would never forget it, and that would be her burden for the rest of her life. It certainly would not permit her to settle for anything less, and with Theo, she knew, it would be much, much less. His hands, his lips had been a totally unwarrantable intrusion on her womanhood. She could no more have given him her body than she could have flown to the moon.

It was so unfair, really, she allowed herself to think unwillingly. Theo at least was prepared to offer her an honourable marriage, and she cared nothing for him—was, in fact, a little repulsed by his attentions. Whereas to Devlin, whose slightest touch could send her body flaming with a white-hot craving she could neither explain nor excuse, she was simply the amusement of an hour. Just another in a series of amorous diversions. It hurt, but it had to be faced.

And having faced it, she lifted her head and looked at Mrs Brandon.

'I'm sorry,' she said, 'but I really don't care for Theo—in that way.'

'Is that such an insuperable barrier?' Mrs Brandon's

eyes were narrowed. 'You are very young, my dear, to know your own mind on such a subject, but if you are wise you will not permit it to trouble you unduly. I did not.' She gave a faint smile. 'That—shocks you? But the English are such an impractical nation with their dream of true love. My sister was as bad, marrying a younger son because she fell in love, when the older one was there for the taking.' She leaned forward putting her hand over Christina's. Her fingers felt dry and warm. 'Land, *mon enfant*, property, the continuation of a heritage—those are the important things in marriage. That has never occurred to you, *hein*, because you did not think it could ever happen. But we will not rush you. You shall have time to think—to consider. Now leave me, *ma chère*, I wish to get dressed. You may send Eulalie to me.'

Almost without knowing how it had happened, Christina found herself back in the sitting room. Her head was whirling. What had she got herself into? she asked despairingly as she made her way back to her own room. She had gone to Mrs Brandon that morning, intent on handing in her notice, only to have it waved aside as if it were some momentary aberration. And now she was being slowly but surely pressurised into marrying Theo. The appalling thing was that Mrs Brandon made it all sound so sane and reasonable. Just for a moment, if you were not very careful, you might find yourself thinking that one's objections were very trivial in the light of the broader issues involved.

She closed her bedroom door behind her and leaned back against the panels, trying to regain control of her suddenly shaking limbs. At least, she had been allowed a breathing space. She had time to marshal her arguments, let them see she could not be coerced, however subtly. But it brought home to her even more forcibly that she needed to get away. If she could just get as far as Martinique, she could surely find some sort of work—something that would keep her and enable her to save for her fare home—that is if Mr Frith was unable or unwilling to help her.

The imminent problem was how to get to Martinique. She could, of course, ask Louis to drive her to the harbour where the ferry stopped, but she had to remember that he was in Mrs Brandon's pay and might well report any such request. And though she might tell herself defiantly that she was a free agent and that the Brandons could not stop her leaving, she could not convince herself that this was the whole truth.

She toyed with the idea of appealing to Clive and Lorna Maynard. Lorna would help, she was sure, if she knew what the position was. And yet was it fair to ask her? Clive was also an employee of the Brandon family and it was wrong to expect him to perhaps put his job in jeopardy.

With a groan, she wandered over to the dressing table and sank down on the stool, burying her face in her hands. There was another alternative, of course, an obvious one if she could only bring herself to accept it.

Devlin Brandon had a boat—a boat in which he had presumably sailed single-handed back from Martinique, because he had certainly not been on the ferry with them. More than that, he had made no secret of his wish that she should leave Ste Victoire. Would he be prepared to give the practical help in achieving this end that she so badly needed? Certainly there was no obvious reason why he should deny it. He owed no loyalty to his aunt—he had made that clear.

But she—she was in his debt already. Had she any right to ask him for help? What had he told her? *'Don't come crying to me when things get rough.'* She shivered. Now she was considering doing precisely that, and she would have no one but herself to blame if he turned her away.

She got up stiffly and walked across to the window. He wouldn't turn her away, a little voice inside her was insisting, but he might charge a price for his help—this time. She pressed her hands over her ears, resolutely shutting it out. She couldn't let herself think about that or she might lose her courage altogether.

Without stopping to consider the wisdom of her actions any longer, she slipped out on to the gallery and down the steps to the garden.

She was breathless and her side was hurting by the time the beach house was in sight. She stopped and shaded her eyes, suddenly uneasy. The place had a closed, shuttered look that she did not remember, and then, with a rapidly sinking heart, she noticed something else. *Moon Maiden* was no longer at her mooring.

She paused irresolutely. Her obvious course was to go back to the house and wait for his return, whenever that might be. That was the thing to do, she told herself, even as her feet began to carry her steadily forward again.

The door was shut, but it wasn't locked. Perhaps he wouldn't be gone for long—or maybe he had left some clue as to when he would be back, she argued against her conscience as she pushed the door open and stepped inside.

The shutters were closed, and the air inside hung, heavy and still and full of silence. The shack was obviously empty. Christina made her way over to one of the windows at the far end of the living room, and opened back the shutter, letting the sunlight swarm in, dust motes dancing in its beams.

It was all very neat. There were no unwashed dishes, and in the next room the bed had been tidily made. There was nothing to suggest that the owner had left in a hurry and would soon be back. It was far more indicative of the leisured preparation for a journey. She glanced round a little uncertainly. She wasn't sure what she expected to see —a note, perhaps, with an address or even a telephone number where he could be reached? She knew she was being ridiculous. Devlin Brandon was accountable to no one for his actions. And she had no excuse at all for being here—prying like this, now that this was established. No excuse at all.

As if she was being manipulated by unseen strings, she

turned back towards the work bench. This, presumably, was where Devlin worked at his woodcarving. She was curious, to the point of compulsion, to see the kind of work he produced. He didn't seem to have any samples on open display. She guessed these must be his current works, shrouded by the covering sheet.

Still she hesitated. What would she do—what could she say if he was suddenly to return and find her here like this, so obviously snooping through his things like this? She glanced warily towards the open door, but it was filled by nothing but sunshine and the murmur of the sea.

Feeling like Bluebeard's youngest wife, she lifted the corner of the sheet, and picked up the first carving. It was a bird—some kind of hawk, she thought, but so acutely observed that she half expected it to take flight from her hands as she held it. She was no connoisseur of the medium, but she could recognise artistry when she saw it. His aunt might dismiss his talent with a casual wave of her hand, but that could not diminish it. She looked eagerly at the other carvings. They all seemed to have this same individual mastery of touch—the same vivid life as the hawk.

There was just one more to see. She pulled it free of its wrappings and stared down at it, her mouth suddenly dry. It was a small statuette—a girl kneeling. A typical enough subject, she supposed, and it wasn't even finished. Yet it was unmistakable. The girl was Eulalie, and she was naked. Again, there was nothing in that. All artists used nude models, she supposed. But it was the way she was posed— on her knees, arms slightly extended. Every line of that voluptuously bare body sang surrender—an offering which no virile man could have either mistaken or refused.

Her hands shaking, she put the figure down. How many times, she found herself wondering, had Eulalie been here for this to be achieved? Her mind went back to that first night at Archangel when she had seen the girl creeping off through the garden. Her guess as to her destination had been right, it seemed. But it hadn't mattered then—or at least not much. It shouldn't matter now. She ought to be able to look at the figure quite objectively as if she had looked at the others and assess its artistic value. Devlin would have little trouble in selling this, she told herself, trying to be casual. It was an utterly sensuous piece with a delicate eroticism all its own. A woman's body carved in wood by a man who knew it well.

She felt hot tears burning at her eyelids—a kind of tormented rage welling up hysterically inside her. My God, she thought, I'm jealous. It was nonsense. It was ludicrous. She had no right—no reason. He had kissed—more than kissed her once—that was all. At all other times they had been adversaries. With a little choking sob, she turned and ran for the door, scrubbing furiously at her stinging eyes with a scrap of handkerchief as she went, and thrusting it wildly back into her pocket before slamming the door behind her.

Today she had learned something about herself. Something unpalatable but a fact nevertheless. Somehow, she had fallen in love with Devlin Brandon.

She shook her head violently in repudiation as she stumbled along the beach. It wasn't love—it couldn't be. She had too much sense to confuse liking and tenderness and respect with the sheer physical desire that Devlin aroused in her. It was a primitive—an animal thing—and she wasn't like that.

She wasn't, she repeated agonisedly, she wasn't. And found she was still saying the same phrase over and over again like an incantation all the way back to the comparative sanctuary of her room at Archangel.

For the next two days, Christina felt that she was existing in a kind of limbo. Her duties for Mrs Brandon had never been onerous; now they were practically non-existent. She was expected to appear at meals, and little else. Theo was on his best behaviour. She could recognise this and almost be amused by it. She had forced herself to endure his emotional apology for his behaviour the other night and had made it clear that she expected no repetition of it. He had reverted to being the undemanding companion again, only a little more anxious to please. She accepted his attentions with an indifference which only seemed to prompt him to exert himself more. He obviously felt he was on the shortest road to her good graces, and there seemed little point in disillusioning him.

It was strange how the worry over her developing relationship with Theo had retreated from the forefront of her mind under the impetus of this new and shattering discovery. Yet it all came to the same thing in the end— she had to get away from here. All she needed was the means.

She could no longer turn to Devlin for help. That would be like rubbing salt in a self-inflicted wound. The only thing that would preserve her peace of mind would be to make her escape while he was still away. From the security of the adjoining cove, she could make sure that *Moon Maiden* was still missing from the mooring. While he was gone, she felt absurdly safe as if, on his return, one glance at her face would tell him all she was so desperately trying to conceal.

Her thoughtfulness, her pallor and the shadows under her eyes might have been remarked by Mrs Brandon, but they were not commented upon. Perhaps her employer felt she was merely making heavy weather of considering her options. There was an air of almost tangible satisfaction about the older woman these days as if it was only a matter of time before all her designs were accomplished and she knew it.

Sometimes, Christina allowed herself a wry smile. If Mrs Brandon really knew! she thought. But it was just as well she didn't, or her position here would be truly untenable.

The hardest thing of all to bear was the presence of

Eulalie, she found. Christina wondered if she was being over-sensitive, but there seemed to be an air of secret knowledge, of triumph almost in the girl's demeanour these days—especially when she came anywhere near herself. With Mrs Brandon she presented her usual demure, submissive appearance. It was as if she guessed the unhappy secret that Christina nursed and was exulting over her. There was an extra sway to her hips and a thrust to her full breasts whenever she entered Christina's room. She seemed to be flaunting her exotic beauty—reminding Christina, if she needed any such reminder, of how intimately it had been displayed at the beach house for Devlin Brandon's delectation.

Once she had even entered the bathroom while Christina was taking a shower, even though the sound of the running water must have warned her that the room was occupied. She had apologised instantly and withdrawn, but Christina had been aware of and embarrassed by her swift but thorough appraisal of her slender contours, and left with the humiliating thought that Eulalie had been comparing her unfavourably with her own lush curves.

Yet it was all covert. There was nothing at all in Eulalie's attitude that Christina could have complained of, even had she been so minded. She had always known that the girl resented having to wait on her, but that hardly mattered as she intended to leave.

But how? She had resigned herself to the fact that she could not leave until she had received her first salary cheque, and that was not due yet. She could not very well ask for an advance, because Mrs Brandon was quite aware that she had had no expenses to speak of. Besides, it would not be right. She would not leave in the Brandons' debt. There must be no strings attaching her still to Archangel once she had gone from Ste Victoire.

Somehow she would have to transfer herself and her belongings from the house to the harbour at La Villette to catch the boat for Martinique, even if she had to summon one of the few local taxis to take her instead of slipping away as she wished. But here there was another difficulty. The only outside telephone was situated in Mrs Brandon's sitting room, and the chances of making a call unobserved were few and far between. Christina sighed. That was another bridge she would have to cross when she came to it.

She had just returned from her walk on the beach one morning, having ascertained that *Moon Maiden* still had not returned, when Mrs Brandon sent for her. Although it was still relatively early, Christina found that she was up and dressed and sitting at the elegant desk in her sitting room. There was a brisk almost excited air about her.

'Come in, *ma chère*. There is a lot for us to do today.' She held out a long handwritten list of what appeared to be names and addresses. 'You will find a box of envelopes in that drawer. Type them quickly, please. The invitations arrived from the printer this morning and I wish them to go out without delay.'

'Invitations?' Christina picked up the list and studied it. Practically all the island's notables appeared to be on it.

'*Oui*. It is Theo's *jour de fête* next week—his birthday— and naturally we shall have a celebration—a small party.'

Christina's brows rose slightly. If this was a small party, she would have liked to have known Mrs Brandon's idea of a large one. But as she read down the list of names, one omission leaped out at her. Devlin's name was not there. She had no doubt this was quite deliberate, a way of signifying his aunt's displeasure with him, yet it seemed unfair when his colleagues on the island committee such as Ludo Bellairs and his family were being invited.

'I'll get on with it immediately, *madame*.' She turned towards the door.

'*Un moment*.' Mrs Brandon's voice halted her. Christina looked back and saw that she was sitting, twisting her fountain pen in her fingers as if she was suddenly nervous about something. 'Christina—it would please me greatly if the party were not merely to celebrate Theo's birthday but also his engagement.'

Christina's heart felt like a stone inside her. She suppressed a groan. She had foolishly hoped that any further discussion on the subject could be avoided for the duration of her stay at Archangel.

She tried to temporise. 'Madame, you said I should have time to think—to consider . . .'

'But what is there to consider?' Mrs Brandon's eyes fastened on hers. There was a strange appeal in them. 'And you must have thought it over by now. Theo is young—headstrong. He will not wait for ever for his answer while you debate with yourself.'

'I don't want him to wait,' Christina said obstinately. 'I—I can't marry him, Mrs Brandon. I don't love him.'

'But you could learn.' The older woman's eyes seemed to burn into hers. 'What else, after all, is an engagement for but to enable two people to get to know each other—to grow from friends to lovers. Theo has kept his distance in accordance with your wishes, but—if you were promised to each other—it would be a simple matter, living in the same house as you do, for him to teach you to care for him.'

Christina stared at her, her brain reeling. 'I don't know what you mean,' she managed eventually.

'Oh, come, *mon enfant*,' Mrs Brandon's tone was chiding. 'You must not be coy. I am saying that when two young attractive people live in close proximity there will naturally come a time when their emotions may—overwhelm them. If you were to—belong to Theo completely, your feelings might well undergo a change.'

Christina felt sick. 'I'm sorry if you regard me as merely being coy,' she said, trying to keep her voice calm. 'But I have no intention of—sleeping with Theo. Whether I was engaged to him or not wouldn't make the slightest difference.'

'I have shocked you, I see,' Mrs Brandon gave a rather

negligent shrug of the shoulders. 'Forgive me. It seemed an eminently practical solution.'

Christina closed the door firmly behind her and leaned against it for a moment, closing her eyes in utter disbelief. Not for the first time, she found herself totally bewildered by the fact that this woman had been Aunt Grace's friend. Certainly they had not seen each other for years, but did people really change all that much? She just could not imagine how Aunt Grace would have tolerated for a moment someone so apparently amoral as Marcelle Brandon. Her own life had been conducted on lines of quite rigid principle, instilled in her since girlhood. Unless Mrs Brandon had been a consummate actress, Aunt Grace must surely have seen that her friend had feet of clay.

She walked down to the library and set about the task of typing the envelopes. But her fingers were all thumbs and she found that her usual accuracy had deserted her. With a groan she ripped another spoiled envelope out of the carriage and screwed it into a ball before hurling it towards the open window.

'Good shot.' The last voice in the world she had expected to hear spoke in mocking approval from the doorway behind her. 'Beware, Miss Sort-of-Secretary. Your halo would appear to be slipping.'

She sat very still, resisting the immediate impulse to turn and look at him, aware that a tide of betraying colour was sweeping up into her face.

Devlin strolled across the room and stood beside her, looking down at the creased list lying beside the typewriter. 'So Tante is having one of her rare bouts of sociability,' he remarked, raising his eyebrows sardonically. 'Don't bother to type an envelope for me, Miss Bennett. I'll take my invitation with me.'

She picked up another envelope and wound it into the machine. 'I don't think you're being invited,' she told him woodenly.

He didn't seem put out in the slightest. 'Then I shall

gatecrash. This is one Archangel party I wouldn't miss for the world. I want to be there when Theo puts the Brandon ring on your finger. Have you seen it yet, by the way? It's an enormous emerald flanked by diamonds—vulgarity personified.'

The letters being formed under her fingers were sheer gobbledygook, but she went on typing steadily. 'For the last time,' she said between her teeth, 'I am not getting engaged to Theo.'

'No?' He threw himself into a chair, stretching his long legs out in front of him. 'That's not what's being whispered all over the island. But perhaps you never listen to gossip.'

She paused uncertainly, her fingers poised over the keys. 'People are saying . . .?'

'That you're on the verge of being married off to Theo —yes.' There was no mockery now in the silver eyes. They were sombre, almost brooding. 'This party will simply be regarded as the seal on the contract.'

'But it's not true,' she said with a kind of quiet desperation.

He shrugged, his eyes resting on her taut, unhappy face. 'Perhaps it will be—by the time of the party. When's it being held? Theo's birthday? That's just over a week— plenty of time for a determined woman like Tante to achieve her own way. You're not still denying, I hope, that it's her intention to marry you to Theo?'

'No,' she said in a low voice, her head bent. 'But I didn't know—when I came here . . . you must believe me.'

'Oh, I do—for what it's worth.' He took a pack of cheroots from his pocket and lit one. 'What I want to know is what you intend to do about it.'

'Do?' She took the envelope out of the machine and laid it to one side.

'Why, yes,' he sounded impatient. 'I do have a vested interest in all this, you know.'

'I don't see how . . .' she began, and then light dawned.

'Oh, of course! If Theo marries and has a child, then that would put you right out of the inheritance.'

There was a long silence, and then he uttered a brief, mirthless laugh.

'Clever girl!' His voice was cynical. 'You catch on fast. Yes, I do have my reasons for preferring Theo to remain single. Do I have your co-operation in helping to achieve that entirely laudable aim?'

'I've already told you I have no intention of marrying Theo.' Her throat seemed to be hurting her oddly. 'You—you have nothing to fear from me in your—plans.'

'I'm delighted to hear it,' he said drily. 'And how do you intend to escape the fate that Tante has it all mapped out for you?'

'Oh,' she shrugged vaguely, 'I do have one or two little schemes in mind. You really don't have to worry.'

'Oh, but I do,' he said softly. 'Particularly if I happen to be involved in any of them.'

Her eyes flew to his with something like panic. 'You're not,' she said quickly.

'No?' He stood up and walked over to her. For a moment he looked down at her, then he reached into the pocket of his dark grey corded pants. 'Yours, I believe,' he said lightly, and dropped something into her lap. It was a handkerchief, small and lace-trimmed and entirely unremarkable but for the betraying embroidered 'C' in one corner. Her hand closed round it.

'Where—where did you find this?'

'Don't you remember? Or were you in too much of a hurry to leave?' His hand reached down and took her chin, remorselessly forcing her face up to meet his glance. 'Don't pretend, Christina. You came to the beach house while I was away in Martinique. I knew someone had been there because a shutter had been left open and it was obvious someone had been having a sneak preview of some of the exhibits for my next show. I realised it was you when I found your handkerchief on the floor. I couldn't quite swallow the premise that it was a burning interest in my prowess as a woodcarver which had brought you there, so it occurred to me you might have needed my help. Am I right?'

She sat very still, then she managed a shaky laugh. 'It's very kind of you to offer me a way out—but I'm afraid it's much simpler than that. Sheer feminine curiosity, and quite unforgivable, I know. You were away—and I was dying to have a look round, so I just walked in ...' Her voice tailed away, then rallied. 'I—I shall have to cover my tracks more carefully next time.'

'I see,' he said expressionlessly. His fingers fell away from her chin and she touched her flesh uncertainly, wondering if he had bruised her. 'I'm sorry I wasn't there to entertain you in person. I might have been able to satisfy your curiosity on several other points as well.'

There was no mistaking the implication in his words, and Christina's face burned. 'I'm sorry too. Sorry I ever went near the place,' she said in a constricted voice. She tried to get up, but his hand caught at her shoulder, pressing her down into her seat. Her eyes dilated as she looked up at him.

'Sit still,' he said roughly. 'I haven't finished with you yet.'

'Oh, please!' Her voice trembled. 'I've apologised. What else can I say?'

'To hell with words.' His tone was even, but she could hear the suppressed anger underneath it. 'You've invaded my privacy, my dear Miss Bennett, so it's only fair that you should suffer a similar invasion.' As he spoke, he sank down on to the chesterfield beside her, his hand moving from her shoulder to tangle in the soft honey mass of her hair.

She tried to say 'Devlin', but her voice broke in the middle of the word and then his mouth was on hers and her chance to protest was gone. She felt as if she was drowning in delight. An agonising sweetness pierced her innermost being as he drew her against him. One hand stroked the nape of her neck, the other moved on her back softly and caressingly, freeing the flimsy material of her shirt from her waistband. His fingers were cool and deliberate on her warm skin, spreading along her spinal column, finding the hook fastener that was the final barrier to his seeking touch and dealing with it effortlessly. She gasped as she realised what he had done and tried to pull away, but his grip tightened ruthlessly, and she lay pliant again in his arms, her breath coming raggedly.

For a moment he lifted his mouth from hers, and his eyes seemed to pierce her face. Then, as if satisfied with what he had found, he bent to her again, his kiss deepening and demanding more response than she had ever dreamed she was capable of. Time stood still as his long, leisurely, frankly intimate exploration of her mouth and body continued. She was unable to think coherently. She was all sensation, all awareness, and she gave a little broken sigh of pleasure as his lean, hard fingers tantalised the softness of her breasts.

Her head fell back across his arm like a broken flower as his lips slid down her throat and lightly brushed her shoulders before discovering for themselves the sweet excitement his touch had aroused. She heard herself moan faintly as the warmth of his mouth woke new hungers in her. His fingers lingered caressingly on her rib cage, then slid lower to the waistband of her skirt. As if she was in a dream, she felt the button which held it give way. And then it was all different. He was still holding her, but his mouth was no longer rousing her to feverish intoxication.

Dazedly she opened her eyes and looked up into his face. He thrust up a hand and raked back some strands of tawny hair, damp with sweat, from his forehead. His breathing was uneven, and his body held a sudden tension as if he had himself rigidly in check.

He saw her watching him, and his mouth twisted cynically. 'Well, Christina? Have you learned your lesson—or do we proceed to the next step?'

Insultingly casual, his hand returned to the zip of her skirt. His eyes never left her face. For a moment, she could hardly take in what he had said, and then with a little cry she flung herself away from him, dragging her unfastened shirt over her breasts.

'I suppose I have my answer,' he said after a slight pause. He stood up and started to straighten his own dishevelled appearance.

She stared up at him, her eyes blurred with shamed tears. 'I hate you,' she whispered unsteadily.

He laughed softly. 'Then it must be a very cerebral hatred, honey girl. Your body certainly hasn't heard about it.'

Her hands were shaking as she re-fastened her clothes, thrusting the buttons through holes that seemed in some strange way to have become far too small to accommodate them.

'Do you need any help?'

'Don't you dare to touch me!' she breathed.

'There's no "dare" about it,' he said tautly. 'If I wanted to touch you again, I would, and there'd be damn all you could do about it. You know it, and so do I. But this is neither the time nor the place. I have to see my aunt—and you have to finish typing those envelopes, although I wouldn't give much for their chances of getting in the mail today.'

'Oh, get out!' she cried passionately, burying her face in her hands. She did not move until she heard the library door close quietly behind him.

# CHAPTER SEVEN

CHRISTINA removed the last envelope from the typewriter and placed it on the completed pile. She checked through the list to make sure that no one had been missed, then sat back with a sigh, stretching her arms wearily and flexing her shoulder muscles. It might look like a pile of envelopes, but she knew it was really a major victory for applied concentration. Her head might ache, and her body might be damp with sweat, but she felt that she had won out over her own weakness.

She picked up the pile of envelopes and the list to take them upstairs to Mrs Brandon, then hesitated. For all she knew, Devlin might still be with his aunt, and she could not face seeing him again so soon. Not now. Not while she still ached with the frustrated longings he had so cynically roused in her.

Her sole consolation was that Devlin would never know how successful his so-called punishment had been. All he knew was that he could make her respond to him physically—but then he was an experienced man dealing with an inexperienced girl, so he would probably expect that. What he did not know was how deeply her emotions were involved. At least she did not have that self-betrayal to regret when she left Ste Victoire behind her for ever. There was a chance—just a chance—that she might still be able to take her departure with a little dignity left.

She got up and wandered over to the open window. Her clothes felt clammy on her, and she thought with longing of the swimming pool. There was no reason, of course, why she should not go for a bathe. She had finished her appointed task, and her time was presumably her own again.

133

She did not hesitate for a moment longer but ran up to her room and changed into a bikini narrowly striped in dark green and white, then, grabbing a towel, made her way down the gallery stairs to the poolside.

The water felt glorious. She swam lazily from one end to the other, then turned on to her back and floated, her hair streaming on both sides of her in the water. She began to feel refreshed, and decided that strenuous physical exercise had been just what she needed. She swam another couple of lengths, then hauled herself out and sat on the side, drying her hair on the towel. Then she applied sun oil liberally to her arms and legs and lay down on one of the padded loungers to sunbathe. It was very quiet. Archangel could have been peopled by mutes. The only sound came from insects buzzing in the flowers and grasses, and in the distance a bird called raucously. Christina found her thoughts drifting drowsily, and made no effort to jerk herself back to wakefulness. Perhaps, when she woke, the pain would be gone, she told herself sleepily.

But her dreams as she slept were wild and disturbing with a quality of nightmare about them. Wooden figures grew and came to life—a boat sailed away and left her alone and desolate on the shore. A storm brewed and lightning flashed with the rumble of thunder in the distance. It was raining too—big icy drops which fell vindictively on to her bare skin as she tried unavailingly to shelter ...

She opened her eyes and found that the drops were real. Theo was standing over her, sprinkling her with a handful of water from the pool. She sat up unwillingly, conscious of his eyes appreciatively on her scantily clad body. He had kept away from the pool over the last few days, but today he was wearing his usual brief trunks and had a towel slung over his shoulders, so she guessed he had decided the time was ripe for him to try and get back on the old terms with her.

'Thank you for waking me,' she said quickly, reaching

for her own towel. 'It's time I was going in. Your grandmother will be wanting me.'

'Grand'mère doesn't want anyone today.' Theo scowled slightly. 'She has had Devlin with her all morning. I know these sessions of old. She will be in a terrible temper for the rest of the day and will probably insist on having all her meals in her room. So you and I will have to make the best of it together, my sweet.' He spread his towel on the flags beside her lounger and lay down.

'All the same, I ought to be going ...' she began, but he put out a hand and took hold of her ankle.

'Don't leave me, Tina,' he said plaintively. 'You're surely not holding the other night against me still?'

'Of course not,' she assured him too quickly.

He smiled up at her. 'Then stay for a little while. Swimming pools are dull places without a beautiful girl beside them. And I do find you very desirable, you know.'

'If you're going to talk like that, Theo, then I shall go indoors,' she said, irritated.

He sighed petulantly and let go of her. He rolled on to his back and lay staring up at the sky.

'Devlin would have to come today,' he remarked sulkily. 'Just when Grand'mère was making the arrangements for my party. I was hoping this afternoon to take her to look at my boat.'

'Boat?' Christina turned and looked down at him questioningly. He nodded eagerly.

'My birthday present,' he said. 'Oh, it's beautiful, Tina —far better than Devlin's *Moon Maiden*. Bigger too. It's tied up at Fort Victoire at the moment—just waiting for Grand'mère to sign the papers.' The moody look returned to his face. 'Of course, now she may refuse.'

'I hardly think that's likely,' Christina said drily. 'You seem to get your way in most things.'

'Yes.' He sent her a speculative look under his lashes. 'Except in the one thing I want most.' His voice changed, became lighter, almost laughing. 'Come with us to see the boat, Tina. She's a lovely thing—perfect for a honeymoon. I might even call her after you.'

'I don't think that's a good idea,' she said tightly, and sat up.

'Now I've upset you again.' He gave a gentle sigh. 'You are so touchy, Tina. Don't run away, I promise to be good —that is if you'll answer me one question.'

'What is it, Theo?' she said wearily.

'Why don't you want to marry me?' His tone was frankly curious. The golden boy, she found herself thinking sadly, the top prize in the competition unable to understand why he hadn't been won yet. She wished she had stuck to her guns and gone back indoors. She tried to temporise.

'We—we can't dictate our feelings, Theo. It's hard to explain, but ...'

'You just don't want me,' he said gently. He turned his head and smiled at her. 'Go on, Tina. Be frank. I can take it.'

'It—it's not as simple as that,' she began stiltedly. 'I don't want anyone ...'

'No?' His smile widened slightly. 'That's not what anyone passing the library window this morning would have thought.'

She lay very still, loathing the betraying colour she could feel flooding into her face.

'Oh, Tina,' he gave an exaggerated sigh. 'Another scalp for my Cousin Devlin's belt—and he has far too many already. Don't worry, I won't give you away to Grand'mère. And I'm not the jealous type, you know. Once we were married, I wouldn't mind you having—the odd diversion— as long as you were discreet, of course.'

She was more appalled by that than by anything he or Mrs Brandon had ever said to her before.

'You can't be serious!'

'Why not?' he shrugged. 'It could be very entertaining.

I wonder how dear Devlin's pride would stand sharing a woman with me—knowing that he might be contributing another little Brandon to stand between him and Archangel.' He looked quizzically up into her horrified face and flung back his head in a shout of laughter, displaying his perfect teeth. 'My God, Tina, I think you really took me seriously for a moment. You're deliciously easy to shock, you know. Come on,' he rose to his feet in one easy, graceful movement, 'let's go for a swim together and forget all this nonsense. You may not want me as a lover, but we can still be friends.'

She yielded unwillingly to his urging. Perhaps she was too easily shocked, she thought, as he tugged her towards the edge of the pool, but she hadn't thought that he was joking. There had been a bite in his words that had really got under her skin.

Their bodies cut the water together, and they began to swim the length of the pool side by side. Theo seemed to be holding back, matching his stroke to hers, showing a consideration which surprised her. When they had swum together on previous occasions he had always seemed anxious to demonstrate his superior strength and expertise, making her feel like a clumsy schoolgirl in the water.

'Race you!' he called out, and Christina smiled inwardly as she quickened her stroke. That was more like the Theo she had come to know. Which made it all the more surprising when she found she was actually in the lead. She had no illusions about her swimming. She was competent in the water, no more, whereas Theo had probably learned to swim almost as soon as he could walk. With a feeling of unreality, she touched the end of the pool, lifting her hand in triumph.

Theo surfaced beside her. 'Well done!'

'You let me win,' she accused.

'Nonsense.' He splashed her playfully, and with a gasp she retaliated. The air was full of flying droplets. Her ears

were singing and instinctively she closed her eyes against
the barrage. When it stopped, she opened them tentatively.

'Theo?'

There was no reply. She glanced up at the edge of the
pool where the towels were, half expecting that he had
climbed out to dry himself, but he was nowhere to be seen.

Then suddenly something grabbed at her legs, dragging
her down into the vivid turquoise depths of the water. She
gasped in surprise, swallowing water. She fought free of
the grip round her legs and surfaced again.

'Theo, you brute . . .'

Her words were cut off as she was dragged down again.
She'd had barely time to draw breath and she didn't—she
really didn't—enjoy being ducked. She was no water-baby.
Above her head was sunlight and air and that was where
she wanted to be. She thrashed around wildly, trying to
kick her legs free, holding her breath with determination. If
Theo got hurt, he would only have himself to blame, she
thought grimly.

It was beginning to get uncomfortable—her lungs were
aching, and she redoubled her efforts to free herself. Suddenly it was no longer a game. It was a fight—a bid to
establish some kind of supremacy—not physical, Theo had
no need to do that. He was stronger than her and always
would be, his muscles tempered by his swimming and
riding. This was a duel to show her who was the master.

She was frightened, of course she was, but her predomin-
ating emotion was one of anger.

Don't panic, she adjured herself. That was the important thing. They couldn't stay down there for ever. Theo
would have to breathe eventually. All she had to do was
remember that.

But it was becoming difficult to remember anything besides her own obsessive need to draw breath. Her head was
pounding and she felt as if something inside her was going
to burst. His grip round her legs showed no signs of slack-

ening, no matter how much she twisted and wriggled.

No one, she found herself thinking with absolute clarity, no one was allowed to reject Theo Brandon with impunity. All that charm, that apparent good humour was just a cloak for an ego that you wounded at your peril. And she had rejected him twice, so now she was being punished, taught a lesson, shown who was boss. And she was damned —damned if he was going to get away with it!

It was hard to stick to her resolution, particularly when she knew that only a few inches above her head was blessed, blessed air, and that all she had to do in order to get it was meekly submit. Her muscles were aching now, and her whole body felt as if it had been stretched on the rack. She was almost at the point where it was impossible to fight any more. Almost, but not quite.

Suddenly her arms were being wrenched from their sockets as well as her legs, and she groaned aloud, choking as the water rushed into her mouth. There was an intense glowing brightness, but even as she lifted her face towards it gratefully, the darkness came down and smothered her.

Somewhere someone was retching, a harsh painful sound. It felt painful too—like a great fist twisting in her stomach —pressing down on her back, forcing the water out of her. With a moan she opened her eyes. She was lying face downwards on a pile of towels at the side of the pool. The pressure on her lungs increased, and she choked up more water.

Memory came flooding back, and she tried to turn to see whose hands were upon her.

'Lie still,' said Devlin, his voice grim. 'You'll be all right.'

'Tina.' Theo's voice. 'Oh, Tina, my darling!' He dropped to his knees in front of her, his hands cupping her face. 'I'm so sorry, I didn't realise you were in difficulties. It was all a game—only a game.'

There was remorse in his voice, and it might even be sincere. But there was a veiled note of triumph too, and Christina knew that if it was a game Theo was leaving her in no doubt as to who had won. She closed her eyes to shut out the sight of him.

'Can you walk?' Devlin again. Lips tautly compressed, he watched her struggle on to her knees. 'Here, then.' She was lifted up into his arms, cradled against his chest. This time there was nothing loverlike in his touch, but there was an odd feeling of security. She could feel his heart beating under her cheek, hear him asking Theo with chilling abruptness for directions to her room, and Theo's sullen reply.

She kept her eyes closed until she felt herself laid none too gently on the softness of her own bed. When she opened them, Devlin was emerging from the bathroom with her bathrobe and a large towel.

She struggled up on to one elbow, her eyes enormous. 'How . . .?'

'Don't try to talk,' he said. 'Don't try to do anything. Just be still.'

And still she was, while he stripped the sodden bikini from her and dried her briskly with the towel he had brought. Once—a lifetime ago—she had burned with shame because he had touched her skin. Now she lay mute with gratitude under his hands, submitting docilely to being wrapped in the bathrobe while he dried her hair.

He did not speak. His touch was as cool and impersonal as a doctor's. When the excess water had been dried from her hair, he picked up the house telephone and with the same abruptness ordered a tray of tea to be brought to her room. Then he sat down on the edge of the bed and gave her a long, hard look.

'Do you usually indulge in such hectic swimming parties?' he inquired levelly. 'If so, I suggest your technique needs improving. If I hadn't arrived when I did, you could have been in trouble.'

She hesitated. A voice inside her was urging her to tell him the truth—to throw herself into his arms and weep out the panicky reaction which was beginning to set in. But she couldn't do that. She knew only too well what she would be inviting if she did. Instead, weary as she was, she had to fight again—a battle that made what had just transpired in the swimming pool seem like an unimportant skirmish, and which, for her own peace of mind, she could not lose.

'We were just—fooling around,' she said at last, tonelessly. 'Theo was ducking me, and things got a bit out of hand. It was my own fault.'

'I wouldn't argue about that,' he said, too smoothly. 'Maybe you should be a little more careful about the games you indulge in. Or at least your choice of partner for these games.'

'Maybe so.' She bent her head wearily, allowing strands of still-damp hair to fall across her face. 'I—I have to thank you again, it seems.'

He put out his hand and brushed her hair back behind her ear. It was the most casual of gestures, but it made her feel alive again, terrifyingly so. She had to fight a treacherous urge to turn her head and kiss the lean hand that stroked back her hair.

Instead, she said icily, 'Please don't do that.'

His eyebrows rose. 'I'm sorry. I suppose this is another game—pretending my touch is abhorrent to you?'

She lifted her chin defiantly. 'Does it have to be pretence? I—I've said I'm grateful to you. Does that give you an excuse to—take advantage of me?'

Not a muscle moved in his dark face. 'I wasn't aware I was doing so.' He got to his feet. 'Your tea should be arriving shortly. Have it with sugar—plenty of it. Do you want me to have them call the doctor?'

She shook her head, an immense weariness possessing her. She very badly wanted to cry, but she would not give way to such weakness in front of Devlin. No matter what it cost, she had to retain what rags of self-respect were left to her. She did not look at him again, and presently she heard his footsteps on the gallery outside, dying away in the distance as he descended the garden stairs, and then and only then she allowed the first scalding tears to trickle down her face.

She was almost composed again by the time the bedroom door opened to admit Madame Christophe with a tray, closely followed by Mrs Brandon, leaning heavily on her stick.

'Christina!' There was a greyish tinge to Mrs Brandon's usually exquisite complexion. 'What is this I hear? There has been some sort of accident in the swimming pool?'

Christina gave her a long level look as she accepted the cup that Madame Christophe handed to her. In spite of the warmth of the sunlit room, she felt chilled to the bone and her stomach was quivering with reaction. The tea was comforting and as she sipped at it, she could feel the interior trembling begin to die away.

'You could say that,' she agreed.

Mrs Brandon paused for a moment, then made a dismissive gesture to the housekeeper.

She pulled a chair forward to Christina's bedside and sat down. Christina saw with astonishment that her hands were shaking.

'*Pauvre enfant*, what a terrible thing to happen! And how fortunate that Theo was there to rescue you.' Her voice wavered slightly on the last words.

Christina set the cup back in the saucer. 'Is that what he's been saying?' she asked caustically. 'Well, that isn't my impression, *madame*. In fact, if Theo hadn't been there, I probably shouldn't have needed rescuing in the first place.'

The older woman gasped and shrank visibly in her chair. There was a bluish look round her mouth and she produced a handkerchief and dabbed nervously at her lips.

'You are—naturally—overwrought, *ma chère*. You don't

know what you are saying. Rest now, and we will talk later.'

'I know exactly what I'm saying,' Christina returned grimly. 'Theo and I had a brief discussion on marriage, and my views didn't please him. So he saw to it that I was made to suffer for them. I suppose I got off lightly in some ways. A few generations back and he would probably have —tied me to the whipping post and given me fifty lashes.'

'*Ma chère* Christina,' Mrs Brandon tried to smile, 'you must make allowances for a young man's—natural disappointment.'

'Oh, I'm so sorry,' Christina said scathingly. 'In all the excitement, that never occurred to me. But you do realise, I hope, that after this, it's quite impossible for me to stay here. I'd like to leave as soon as possible ...'

'Oh, no!' Christina saw with alarm that Mrs Brandon's colour had deteriorated even further. She was breathing heavily, and one hand was pressed to her chest.

She said sharply, 'Mrs Brandon, are you all right?'

Her employer's eyelids flickered open. 'My pills,' she managed weakly. 'Handbag.'

Christina jumped off the bed and found the bag lying near Mrs Brandon's feet. She found the pill box and pressed it into the older woman's hand. There was the usual jug of chilled fruit juice on the bedside table and she poured some into a glass, slopping it in her haste, and gave it to Mrs Brandon. After a few moments her breathing began to quieten and the blueness started to fade from her lips.

Mrs Brandon leaned back in her chair with closed eyes for a while, then she opened them and looked at Christina standing in front of her. She shrugged her shoulders almost resignedly. 'You see how helpless I am? Yet I have not had an attack since you have been here. You see how I have grown to depend on you.'

Christina clutched the bathrobe defensively round her

body. 'But I haven't done anything,' she started to protest.

Mrs Brandon held up a fragile hand. 'You gave me hope, *mon enfant*. I have not much longer to live and it is the wish of my heart to see Theo settled in life. In you, I saw the means to do this. You were that little bit older and so much more mature. You could give him the stability he needs.'

Christina stared at her. 'Mrs Brandon, you can't still be hoping—not after what has just happened—after what I said?'

'But you were not harmed.' Mrs Brandon's tone became firmer. 'He—he just wished to—punish you a little, as you guessed. Already, you see, you know him. Oh, I do not blame you for being angry. Theo is—headstrong. I have allowed him, perhaps, too much his own way. But a sensible wife could do so much to calm these foolish impulses—this temper that sometimes gets the better of him.'

Christina began to feel that she was fighting her way out of a maze. She said, 'You must listen and you must believe me, Mrs Brandon. I will not marry Theo—now or at any time in the future. You'll have to find someone else to cope with his—tantrums. I intend to leave Ste Victoire and go back to England, with or without your permission.'

'Yes.' Mrs Brandon closed her eyes again. 'Perhaps that would be best. I will arrange a flight for you from Martinique. But not yet. Please—Christina—oblige me in this one last thing. I am not well and there is Theo's birthday party next week to arrange. Please stay until the party is over and I will put no further obstacles in your way. Indeed, I will help you all I can.'

Christina sat down limply on the edge of the bed. After all, she reasoned with herself, it was only a few more days, and at least Mrs Brandon seemed to have accepted the situation.

'And Theo will not be here,' Mrs Brandon went on persuasively. 'I am buying him a boat for his birthday and I have arranged a short cruise on it beforehand. So there will be nothing to cause you the slightest disturbance.'

Oh no, Christina thought ironically, nothing at all. She bit back a sigh.

'Very well, Mrs Brandon,' she said at last, 'I'll stay. But only until the party is over.'

Tossing restlessly in bed that night, she told herself she was being a fool. Mrs Brandon had not hesitated to mislead her in the past. Who was to say that her apparent heart attack had not been simulated as so much else had been? Wouldn't she do better to cut her losses—take the ferry to Martinique and play it by ear from there?

She sat up, punching her pillow into shape. In spite of everything that had happened, she still felt a certain sense of obligation to Mrs Brandon, and she could not forget either that she had been Aunt Grace's friend. I owe her these few days, she told herself, turning on to her stomach and burying her face in the pillow.

Liar, a warning voice whispered deep inside her. You'd have been gone by now if it were not for *him*. He's the real reason you want to stay, even though you know it's hopeless. You're hanging on, hoping for one kind word—but it will never come. He has no kindness for you. You're just an obstacle in his way—the bride his aunt has drummed up for Theo. He wants to be rid of you, and he doesn't care what means he uses. He's made love to you, but don't fool yourself that it means anything. Don't be deceived by what he did for you earlier—he would have done the same for any half-drowned animal. And he's a Brandon, like the others. He uses people too when it suits him. He's used Eulalie. Do you think he would treat you any differently if you were such a fool as to put yourself into his power again? She shuddered convulsively, dragging the bedclothes closer round her.

The morning found her listless and still tired. She dressed quickly, dragging on jeans and a tee-shirt, and made her way to Mrs Brandon's suite. But it seemed that her employer's attack had been genuine enough. The doctor was with her, Eulalie reported abruptly, and Madame would not be getting up that day. She was being ordered to rest.

Christina sighed as she turned away. She had her orders —to prepare for Theo's birthday party. Her first task was to ensure that all the invitations were dispatched, the second to confer with Madame Christophe. The housekeeper was her usual dignified self, and she made no attempt to unbend while she answered Christina's diffident questions. Christina gathered from her attitude that such parties were a welcome rarity at Archangel, and apart from agreeing to send the cook to Christina so that a buffet menu could be discussed, she was not a great deal of practical help.

Christina was beginning to feel quietly desperate when she heard a car draw up outside the house, and Madame Christophe admit a visitor. She imagined it was a caller for Mrs Brandon and was surprised when the library door opened and Lorna Maynard was ushered into the room.

'Lorna!' She got up with a smile. 'What a lovely surprise. Were you passing, or . . .?'

'Hardly.' Lorna's answering smile was constrained. 'One hardly "drops in" at Archangel. No, I received a message summoning me here first thing this morning. I understand I have to help you get ready for a party.'

'I see.' Christina felt troubled. Lorna was being civil enough, but she could sense there was real annoyance underneath. 'What have you done with the children?'

'Left them with Seraphine,' Lorna answered shortly. She came over to the table where Christina was working, and studied some of the lists she was making. 'How far have you got?'

'Not very far,' Christina said slowly. 'Lorna, it's very good of you to come here like this.'

Lorna gave her a dry look. 'You would think I had a choice,' she said, then turned back to the lists. 'Is there going to be dancing? You'll need to hire a band. The notice is short, of course. but you shouldn't have any trouble as it's for the Brandons ...'

'Lorna,' Christina put a hand on her arm, 'I don't know what's going on, but you're obviously very sore about something. Please tell me what it is?'

Lorna bit her lip. 'I should be used to it,' she said rather wearily. 'Someone at the big house speaks and we all jump. I have to drop all my plans for the day—and I did have some. I'm not just making a fuss for the sake of it—and come running here to help out "the young mistress".'

Christina sank limply back on the sofa. 'You're joking,' she said helplessly after a minute.

Lorna stared at her. 'I can assure you I'm not. Now, can we get on?'

Christina shook her head. 'Just a minute—it's important. Did someone use those actual words "the young mistress"?'

'Well, of course.' Lorna paused in the middle of rummaging in her bag for a pen and gave her an astonished glance. 'It's not supposed to be a secret, is it, Christina— I mean, this is what the party's all about?'

'No—no, it isn't,' Christina said slowly. Her brain was whirling. She remembered what Devlin had said about her forthcoming engagement being the talk of the island. 'I mean, it isn't what the party's all about. As far as I'm concerned it's simply for Theo's birthday.'

Lorna gave her a frankly sceptical look. 'Then as far as he's concerned, his major present is going to be you. We've all been expecting it ever since you appeared in Fort Victoire together. Everyone gathered from that that Madame Marcelle had given you her blessing.' She flushed slightly. 'I'm sorry, I shouldn't refer to her like that in front of you.'

Christina's eyes met hers steadily. 'You can refer to my —employer in whatever terms you please,' she said. 'After next week, it won't matter at all, because I shan't be here. I'm leaving—going back to England.'

A grin of pure delight spread over Lorna's candid face. 'You mean it? But that's wonderful! To be honest, I wouldn't want to see Theo Brandon within a mile of anyone I was fond of. In my book, he's a spoiled egotistical brat with a temper that will get him in trouble one day. I saw him look at Clive once—he'd corrected him over a small point in front of someone else—and, just for a moment. it was like seeing the devil.'

Yes, Christina thought, it had all been there if she had only had the sense to recognise it. The pride, the passion for power, even the cruelty. But she had been so determined to apply the fortune-teller's warning to Devlin—determined to mistrust him, and to convince himself that he was only warning her against Theo for his own devious ends.

Lorna was still speaking. 'But how are you planning to get away? What the Brandons have, they generally hold.'

'Mrs Brandon promised yesterday that I could leave after the party, and that she wouldn't stop me. In fact, she offered to help.'

Lorna's eyes narrowed slightly. 'From what I know of the lady, I would say that is rather out of character. She doesn't usually accept defeat over her pet schemes with such graciousness. And if she intends you to leave, why is she having the Brandon ring altered?'

'The Brandon ring?' Christina's lips parted in amazement.

Lorna nodded vigorously. 'It came to the bungalow this morning along with the message to me. Clive was to take it to a jeweller in Fort Victoire to be cleaned—and made slightly smaller. A rush job,' she added, her eyes going to Christina's slim fingers.

'I see.' Christina forced a smile. 'What was the plan, I wonder? To present me with a *fait accompli* on the night of the party in the hope that I wouldn't be prepared to make a scene in front of all those people?'

Lorna looked at her gently. 'Well, would you?'

Christina gave a little sigh. 'Probably not,' she said honestly. 'But I would have left all the same—afterwards.'

'Don't underestimate her, Christina,' Lorna advised quietly. 'She may only be a Brandon by adoption, but I don't think they could teach her much about ruthlessness. The fact that you're here at this moment says something about her sheer determination.'

'I can be determined too.' Christina lifted her chin defiantly. 'What time does the afternoon boat leave from La Villette?'

'Four o'clock sharp. But how are you going to get there?'

Christina's eyes danced suddenly. 'I'll get Louis to take me in the car,' she said. 'I've got the perfect excuse. I've heard about a band and I'm going to interview them to see if they'll be suitable for the party.'

'Mm.' Lorna considered the matter with a slight frown. 'But Louis won't just abandon you in La Villette, you know. He'll expect to bring you back.'

'Not if I say I'm meeting you later.' Christina gave her a pleading look. 'I don't want to involve you, Lorna, but you can always say you knew nothing about it. That you also thought I'd gone to interview a band.'

Lorna paused, then appeared to make up her mind. 'I can do more than that,' she said briskly. 'There's the small matter of luggage, of course. You can probably squeeze a nightdress and stuff into your handbag, but what about the rest of your things?'

Christina sighed. 'I shall have to leave them behind, I suppose.'

'Not necessarily,' said Lorna. 'If you can get them packed and downstairs somehow, I can put them in the boot of my car and keep them at the bungalow until you send for them.'

'Would you really?' Christina gave her a grateful look. 'I don't know why you're doing all this for me.'

Lorna gave a slight shrug. 'I have this inborn dislike of seeing people manipulated,' she said quietly. 'When you came to lunch at the bungalow that day, I felt so sorry for you. I was sure, somehow, you had no idea what you were getting into with Master Theo. On the other hand I felt I couldn't warn you, in case I was completely wrong. I had Clive's position to consider. Employees who offend the Brandons have been known to find themselves on a kind of blacklist when it comes to other jobs. And we have two children to think of.' She gave a quick sigh and turned away. 'Now we'd better get on with the party arrangements. That's what we're supposed to be doing, after all.'

By the time lunch—a delicious shrimp and avocado salad followed by fresh fruit—had been eaten, most of the decisions had been made. A detailed room plan had been sketched out, suggesting where the band should be situated, where older guests with no taste for dancing could sit out of earshot, even where the women guests would leave their wraps. As she and Lorna wrangled amicably over which of the blossoms in the garden should be plundered to provide flower arrangements, Christina found herself wondering if in fact the party would be held. Would Mrs Brandon be able to take the loss of face that the abrupt departure of the guest of honour would involve?

When lunch was over, Lorna went off to deal with the cook, and Christina was able to slip away up to her room to start packing.

She felt keyed-up and nervous as she emptied the wardrobe and chest of drawers. Coming to Ste Victoire had been very much a step into the unknown for her and it had proved a near-disaster. By tomorrow she would be on Martinique without a job or the prospect of one, and with very little money to sustain her while she searched for work. It was a demoralising thought. Yet, if she stayed, would she be able to escape the pressure being put upon her to at least become engaged to Theo?

She closed the lid of her suitcase and was beginning to fasten the strap when a sound from behind made her whirl round, her heart thumping.

Eulalie stood just inside the room, her arms full of clean towels for the bathroom, her mouth open with shock. Her eyes were fixed on the suitcase on the bed, and the remaining pile of clothes and other articles waiting to be stowed away in the empty one beside it.

Christina swallowed. Why, oh, why had she not bolted the door? she asked herself frantically. But she had seen no need. The upstairs rooms were all dealt with in the mornings, and it was rare for any of the servants to return there until the evening, when they came to turn down the beds.

Christina suppressed a groan. Eulalie had always disliked her, she knew. It would no doubt give the other girl enormous satisfaction to be able to go to Mrs Brandon and report that her companion was secretly packing for a no-doubt hurried departure. She wondered desperately if it would be possible to bribe Eulalie to keep quiet, but at the same time she knew her already grave financial position precluded any such possibility, even if Eulalie had been willing.

Eulalie spoke first, a grim little smile playing about her lips. 'You are going somewhere, *m'mselle*?'

Christina compressed her lips. 'Don't let's play any cat and mouse games, Eulalie,' she said curtly. 'It's quite obvious, isn't it? I'm leaving. Now run away and tell what tales you have to.'

She had lost all hope of persuading Louis to take her to La Villette now, she realised with a sinking heart. If she wanted to get there for the afternoon boat, it seemed more than likely she would have to walk, carrying her cases. She could not leave them with Lorna now.

'I shall not say anything,' said Eulalie. Christina stared at her in surprise. The other girl's eyes were gleaming, and her tongue passed excitedly over her lips. 'I shall say nothing.'

Christina gave her a steady look. 'I have nothing to give you in return for your silence,' she pointed out quietly.

Eulalie gave a strident laugh. 'Oh, but you are wrong, English girl. You give me everything when you go. You go—and my man will forget about you, and turn back to me. I have seen how he looks at you. I have seen him touch you. But you are prim and cold like all the English. You cannot give him what I give him.'

Pain, that was almost physical, lashed at Christina. She folded her arms tightly across her breasts as if she was trying to protect herself. Of course, for Eulalie it was so simple. Presumably she had been in the vicinity of the library on the previous day and had seen Christina in Devlin's arms, as Theo had done. An image rose in her mind of the carved wooden figure, in all its unashamed longing and passionate surrender. To Eulalie, no doubt, possession was nine points of the law where Devlin was concerned. She had already established her rights, and now the sole threat to them was being removed. No wonder she was making no effort to conceal her delight.

She looked at the overt eagerness on Eulalie's face and compassion assailed her.

'I'm sorry if you've been hurt through me, Eulalie. I never intended it to be so.'

'You hurt no one, m'mselle. Soon, we forget all about you. My man will belong to me again, and it will be as if you never existed.' As she spoke, she snapped her fingers and laughed again.

Christina forced a smile. 'I hope, for your sake, that you're right. But—but is there really any future with a man who is so ready to be unfaithful to you?'

Eulalie gave her a look of contempt. 'Why should he not amuse himself? He is young and a man, non? Too much of a man for you, English girl. Always in the past he has come back to me. But since you came here—not. He will be glad of me when you go. He will be glad to marry me.'

Christina's hands were shaking so violently she could hardly transfer the piles of clothes from the bed to the case. It had never occurred to her that Eulalie would be thinking in terms of marriage. Devlin might be the outcast of the mighty Brandon clan, but surely he would hesitate to commit himself to anyone in Eulalie's position. Unless, she thought achingly, this was to be his final act of revenge against Marcelle Brandon. What price the Brandon pride, when the nephew of the house married his aunt's servant girl?

'You—think he will marry you?' she managed. Sleeping and waking, since her discovery of the woodcarving at the beach house, the thought of Eulalie in Devlin's arms had been hideously at the forefront of her mind. She knew, to her cost, what a demanding lover he would make, and the thought of Eulalie satisfying those demands on a purely physical level had been an agony to her. But his wife! That implied a level of trust, of mental as well as physical intimacy which she would never have guessed existed between them.

Eulalie grinned triumphantly, as if she could read the tenor of Christina's thoughts and was amused by them. 'Oh, I think so, English girl.' For a moment she pressed her hand against her rounded stomach. 'When he knows what I carry.' Her smile widened as she saw how pale Christina had gone. 'You said you had nothing to give me, *m'mselle*. Perhaps I give you something, instead.' Her hand dipped into her overall pocket and came out holding a tightly rolled wad of notes. She tossed it on to the bed beside Christina. 'Take it, English girl. Going away present.'

She left the towels on the dressing table, and walked out of the room.

Christina sank down on to the bed, her legs refusing to

support her any longer. So Eulalie was to have Devlin's child. She supposed it was inevitable, or had it been a deliberate ploy to bind him to her irrevocably? An unbearable picture rose in her mind of Devlin. the cynical lines wiped from his face by a new tenderness as he looked down at the sleeping child in his arms. And it came home to her with all the force of a blow how much she herself wanted to bear him that child.

With a groan, she forced herself to her feet again, dragging her fist childishly across her eyes, refusing to permit the threatened tears to fall. Eulalie had prophesied they would soon forget her once she had departed. Perhaps she also would be able to forget—in time.

She was crazy to feel like this, she told herself vehemently, as she tossed the last few things into her case and closed the lid. They were all still strangers to her—Devlin most of all. She had only been among them a matter of days. Logic insisted that it should not drag the heart out of her to leave. Just because a man with silver eyes and a body as taut as whipcord had held her in his arms, that was no reason to take one wild leap into the realms of fantasy. Devlin Brandon, as she saw him, did not exist. He was merely a myth, manufactured in her mind, a casual rake who helped himself to women as he would take another cheroot. Just another Brandon, exercising a different form of power.

She was well rid of him. She choked back a sob. She was well rid of them all.

She took a last unhappy look around her room, checking that she had forgotten nothing. She had debated with herself whether or not to leave a note for Mrs Brandon, but had decided against it. The pathetic figure who had crouched in the chair beside her bed the previous day might have excited her compassion, but the ruthless manipulator of other people's lives who had deliberately lied to her in order to keep her on the island did not.

She carried her cases down the stairs from the gallery, and round the side of the house, pushing them under a large flowering bush from which Lorna would collect them when the coast was clear. Then she returned to her room to regain access to the main part of the house. As she walked down the big staircase, Lorna was waiting at the bottom with Madame Christophe behind her. Lorna said calmly, 'Louis is bringing the car round, Christina. I told him one of us needed to go to La Villette. Shall we toss for it, or will you volunteer?'

'It's all right.' Christina lifted her chin, hoping she looked more composed than she felt. 'I'll go.'

The minutes of waiting seemed endless. Lorna had tactfully vanished again after giving her a last reassuring smile, and Christina felt very alone suddenly. She walked restlessly over to the front door and stood staring up at the vivid blue sky where some fragile white wisps of cloud floated. She knew she had plenty of time to get to La Villette, but all the same she wished Louis would hurry. It was as if at any moment she expected to see Mrs Brandon coming down the staircase in pursuit. She gave a little shiver and glanced over her shoulder, but she was still alone in the hall. Only the great statue of the Archangel watched her departure. She looked at it uneasily. Was it just her overheated imagination again, or did the towering figure with the upraised spear have a kind of warning about it—as if to remind her that the devil was not yet fully subdued?

She told herself firmly she was being ridiculous, and at that moment, the big grey car rolled to a halt at the foot of the steps.

She was very quiet as the car bumped and lurched its way to La Villette. Louis too was uncommunicative, preferring to whistle softly under his breath as he steered. Christina stared through the windscreen, a prey to her own thoughts. The first thing she would have to do would be to find herself somewhere to stay. She would try and find a small hotel, the sort of place that catered for families, and see if they would allow her to lodge there for a limited period in exchange for her working for them. She would do anything—chamber-maid work, or even help in the kitchens if necessary. Then she would write to Mr Frith, detailing her plight. She had left Eulalie's roll of money where it had landed—on her bed. Let the Brandons make what they would of that, she thought.

It occurred to her suddenly that even allowing for the shortcomings of the road, the car seemed to be behaving rather oddly. Louis tugged at the wheel, frowningly, then pulled the car into the side of the road and got out. When he returned, his face was lugubrious, and he was stripping off his coat. 'Puncture, m'mselle,' he announced, and went to get the tools out of the boot.

Christina concealed a groan. In normal circumstances, they were making good time on the journey, but she had no idea how long it would take Louis to change the wheel, and this could make all the difference. He was certainly start-ing proceedings in a decidedly leisurely manner, as if he had all day ahead of him, and there was no way she could chivvy him along without arousing his suspicion. She got out of the car restlessly and wandered round to watch him at work. She supposed she could not blame him for taking his time. It really was incredibly hot, without even the hint of a breeze.

'Are you going to be very long?' she inquired, trying to sound casual.

Louis shrugged. 'Just as long as it takes, m'mselle,' he returned unhelpfully. Christina turned away, suppressing her irritation with an effort. She walked slowly along the grass verge, looking down over the sheer sprawl of the cliff beneath. Devlin's beach house lay in one of those coves below her, she thought, and found herself wondering what he was doing at that precise moment. Probably out on *Moon Maiden* searching for the elusive wind, she thought.

At least that was a more comforting thought than some that had occurred to her. She turned and strolled back towards the car. Louis did not seem to have made much progress. He seemed to be having trouble in detaching one of the nuts and was swearing softly to himself. Christina maintained a tactful distance, and tried not to glance too obviously at her watch. The precious moments were ticking past at a relentless rate, she saw with alarm, and Lorna had warned her that the boat for Martinique left strictly on time. She looked restlessly up the road, trying to conjure up another vehicle. But if one came, what could she do? What excuse could she fabricate that would convince Louis it was in her best interests to accept a lift to keep an apparently non-urgent appointment rather than wait while he changed the wheel?

She strolled over to Louis and watched his struggles. Should she offer to help?

He glanced up at her, sweat pouring down his brown face. 'Thirsty work, *m'mselle*,' he gasped. 'You go sit in the shade. I be finished here soon.'

But how soon was soon? Christina wondered as time dragged on and little progress seemed to be made. Louis got the wheel off at last and crowed with triumph. Christina felt like joining him. If he hurried now and if they didn't dawdle on the way, they might still get to La Villette in time.

She was careful not to let her impatience show as they got back into the car, and leaned back in her seat with a fair assumption of casualness as if the puncture had merely been a boring setback of a purely transitory nature.

'You keep your fingers crossed, *m'mselle*, that the other old tyre don't go on this devil road,' was Louis' genial adjuration as he started up the engine. Christina closed her eyes for a moment. The prospect was too awful to contemplate.

Every nerve of her body seemed to be jumping with tension as they drove into La Villette and negotiated a careful passage through the crowded streets she remembered so well. Lorna had given her an address not too far from the harbour, which she handed to Louis, telling him briefly that she was meeting Madame Maynard later and would have no further need of his services.

'Yes, *m'mselle*.' Louis gave her a respectful but rather dubious glance as if he doubted her ability to look after herself in the admittedly unsalubrious surroundings of La Villette. Christina supposed that the whisperings about her future position in the Brandon ménage had almost certainly reached the servants' quarters first, and that Louis was only doing what he regarded as his job in guarding—what had Lorna called her?—'the young mistress'.

She got out of the car with an air of confidence she was far from feeling and walked off down the road without looking back and without hurrying. She had checked her watch and she still had a little time in hand, miraculously. She looked back to make sure the car had disappeared, then quickened her steps. She turned the corner, and to her relief, found the harbour was already within sight. It seemed more crowded than she remembered, with every type of boat tied up there. But the ferry was still there—that was the important thing. It was only as she walked along the jetty towards it that she realised there was no gangplank or any other sign of passengers or cargo being taken on board. She increased her pace, gripped by a vague worry. Was it on the point of leaving? Could she still get them to accept her? She began to fumble in her handbag for her purse.

She walked along beside the ferry, staring up at its bulk, but it seemed oddly deserted. Yet if her watch was right, it was just on sailing time. She hesitated, then caught at the sleeve of a passer-by, wheeling a bicycle loaded down with odd-shaped bundles.

'Pardon, *m'sieur*, how does one board the ferry?'

The man grinned at her cheerfully. 'No ferry today,

*m'mselle*. The big wind comes soon. See.' He gestured towards the horizon, and Christina saw to her amazement that the gentle feathery wisps she had noticed earlier had burgeoned somehow and metamorphosed into a great ominous bank of cloud that seemed to threaten thunder and worse things.

'You mean—it's not going to sail? I can't get to Martinique?' Panic made her voice wobble, and the man's smile became reassuring.

'Go home to your friends, *m'mselle*. That's the best place when the big wind blows. But tie your roof on or the devil's breath will whistle it right into the sea.' And he pushed his bicycle away, chuckling.

Christina stood very still in the centre of the wharf. Her heart was thudding so hard it was hurting her. She couldn't get to Martinique. There was just no way. And Louis and the car would be on their way back to Archangel by now. How long, she wondered desperately, would it be before she was missed? Wouldn't it be better to admit defeat now and hire some sort of transport to take her back before the whole flimsy house of cards she had built to mask her departure came tumbling down around her?

She looked at the storm clouds and shivered involuntarily. She wondered how long it would last when it came. One thing was certain—the streets of La Villette would be no place to be when it did arrive. She needed shelter and fast. But where could she hide that the Brandons would not discover? She kicked herself mentally. She had to get a grip on herself. They didn't have supernatural powers— just a modified form of megalomania. All she had to do was keep out of the way until the storm had blown over and the ferry was running again. Surely that wouldn't be too difficult?

She was so lost in thought that she did not hear the approaching footsteps slow down and stop beside her. Her first intimation that she was no longer alone was when a slim well-kept hand descended on her arm in a grip that hurt.

'Well met, Tina,' said Theo Brandon, and he smiled. 'Now whatever are you doing here, *chérie*?'

## CHAPTER EIGHT

CHRISTINA sat slumped in the passenger seat of Theo's sports car, her unseeing eyes fixed on the scenery flying past the window. She was on her way back to Archangel.

There was an air of positive self-congratulation about Theo. There had been little point in trying to maintain the fiction about the band when he had caught her standing on the wharf, staring longingly at the ferry. And the same impending storm which had kept her in harbour had also been responsible for the curtailment of his cruise. There was a terrible irony in that, she thought almost detachedly.

The sky was darkening rapidly and ominouly. She could see lightning flickering on the horizon, and every now and then a gust of wind like the advance guard of some great army seized the car and buffeted it.

'It really isn't very civil, Tina, sneaking away like this.' Theo sent her a darting look. 'I would have thought that silly old woman in England would have taught you better manners than that. Grand'mère said she had. She said that she might be a fool, but she would have taught you to behave.' He heaved a mock sigh. 'She won't be very pleased to be proved wrong.'

Christina closed her eyes wearily. 'Perhaps it will simply convince her that I'm the wrong kind of wife for you. I hope it does.'

'Oh, no.' He smiled and his supple hands tightened perceptibly round the wheel. 'We have no fears on that score. We'll soon be able to—rub off any rough corners that remain, Tina. You're going to be a very important lady.'

'Theo!' Christina made no attempt to hide the appeal in her voice. 'Why does it have to be me? It—it's quite ridiculous. You can't force me to marry you in this day and age.'

He tutted shockedly. 'What a terrible idea! No one's going to force you, Tina. We just hope that if you stay with us a little longer, you'll see things our way. It's an ideal arrangement—you must see that? You need a home and I need a wife.'

'But you don't.' She stared at him wretchedly. 'You're hardly more than a boy. It's years yet before you need to be married.'

He gave a light laugh. 'Life's an uncertain thing, Tina, especially when you have estates—an important heritage to consider. No one expected Uncle Carey and Aunt Madeleine to drown like that—but they did.'

A thought struck her. 'And your parents, Theo? What happened to them?'

His face went completely blank, the smugness, the malice she had glimpsed earlier totally erased.

'That's not important,' he said after a pause. 'It's you and I who are the important ones, Tina. Archangel needs us, don't you see?'

'I see nothing of the sort,' Christina returned. She had slid her hand down beside her and was fumbling for the door catch, but it seemed to be fitted with some kind of safety device because it did not move when she pushed at it. She had some wild notion that if she could open the door, she could jump out as Theo slowed for a bend. But even if she did not actually break an arm or a leg as she jumped, what then? Where could she run to hide—and with the storm gaining on them with every minute that passed.

'There has to be a child,' he said rapidly. 'A child to inherit—if anything were to happen to me. Grand'mère hasn't done what she has done just to see Archangel fall into the hands of that waster—that parasite. Do you know what he'd do with it, Tina? He'd break up the plantation, give it back to the islanders. So I must get married and have an heir. That's why it has to be you. There's no one on Ste Victoire for me to marry. There are girls on Martinique, sure, plenty of them, but there'd be problems. They'd ask too many questions—or their families would, and Grand'-mère doesn't want that. That was why it was so lucky when the old woman in England died when she did.'

Christina wondered dazedly whether she could believe what she seemed to be hearing. That was Aunt Grace he was talking about so callously.

'Stop it!' she pressed her hands convulsively over her ears. 'Have some respect, at least. She was your grand-mother's friend.'

He gave a shout of contemptuous laughter. 'Friend! That's rich. Oh, they were at school together, I grant you that, but there was no love lost between them.'

Christina gazed at him wonderingly. 'Then it was all a lie,' she said slowly and bitterly. 'Every word of it. And she told me that Aunt Grace and she had shared a dream— that their children would eventually marry.'

'Oh, that part of it's quite true,' Theo said negligently. 'That's how Grand'mère found out you existed. The old woman wrote to Tante Madeleine when you went to live with her, highly delighted because she now had the daughter she longed for. But it wasn't me you were intended to marry, chérie, it was Devlin. Grand'mère found the letter among Tante's things when she was sorting them after the funeral. It was Tante Madeleine who was your godmother's great friend, not Grand'mère.'

Christina closed her eyes. She felt physically sick. It seemed she was to be spared nothing—not even the fact that two elderly women had once innocently planned to marry her to the man she most desired in all the world and who was now beyond her reach for ever. She fought back her tears. It was nonsense even to let herself think in terms of 'might-have-been'. Plans and dreams were one thing: reality quite another. No amount of sentimental scheming by anyone could transform Devlin into a tractable bride-groom. How he would laugh if he knew, she thought unhappily.

Theo was speaking again. 'Grand'mère gets a newspaper sent to her from England—a relic of the days when Grand-père was alive. When she saw that Miss Grantham had died, she immediately arranged to set off in search of you. Of course, if you had been ugly or in any way unsuitable, she would not have proceeded in the matter.'

'I wish,' Christina said very clearly, 'that I was cross-eyed, snaggle-toothed and hunchbacked.'

He laughed. 'But you are not, *ma chère* Tina, so we will not discuss such idiocies. You need more flesh, *quant à ça*, for my taste, but our good food will soon see to that.'

'You must stop talking as if I'm going to stay here,' she said. 'I've failed this time, but as soon as I get another opportunity I shall leave. I'm not a sacrificial lamb to be led to the slaughter, you know. And do you really imagine I've forgotten that jolly little game in the swimming pool?'

He shot her an ugly look. 'I don't mean you to forget it. I'm the master at Archangel, my sweet Tina. Perhaps you need another reminder of the fact. I must confess I was surprised at your spirit. I rather like it, in fact, although it has caused some difficulties.'

'Am I supposed to thank you for that?'

He went on as if she had not spoken. 'No, I like a certain amount of fire in a woman. You worried me when you first arrived because you seemed such a timid little thing in some ways. You got very uptight, didn't you, when I telephoned you in your room when you first arrived and you didn't know who it was? And then you told me about what had happened in Martinique and I could see that had upset you too.' He frowned. 'I began to wonder if you had enough courage in you. But that day in the swimming pool, I knew everything would be all right. You'd have drowned sooner than give in to me, wouldn't you?'

'I'm glad the message got through,' she managed. Surreptitiously she wiped her damp palm on her skirt and slid her hand down again to seek the recalcitrant door catch.

Suddenly Theo swung the wheel of the car sharply and it veered across the road. In spite of herself, Christina cried out as the flimsy guard rail which bordered the edge of the cliff appeared in front of them. Then he wrenched at the wheel again, and the car was swerving drunkenly back across the road in the opposite direction.

He laughed triumphantly with more than a touch of malice. 'What's the matter, Tina? Not nervous, are you? There's no need. I know to a centimetre the width of this road, and the car is like part of myself. If we do go through the rail and over the edge it will be because I mean us to. Wouldn't it be tragic—and beautiful. Tina? Can't you just see the headlines in the Ste Victoire *Chronicle*—"Archangel Heir and Bride in Cliff Tragedy"?'

'For the last time, Theo, I am not your bride,' she snapped, her fingers working feverishly at the door catch. 'Now, for God's sake grow up and stop this car before someone gets hurt!'

His laugh was arrogant. 'In my own good time, *chérie*,' he said, and sent the car heading for the cliff-edge again. Christina didn't believe Theo intended to send the car over, but he was flying high and in his condition a fatal mistake would be easy to make.

But this time they were safe. When it seemed the last minute was already past the wheel was spun viciously and the car rocked across the road again. It was a miracle he didn't turn them over, she thought, fighting her panic. It was almost dark now, the sky above flying great streamers of black cloud. Ahead of them a solitary tree loomed stark against the leaden distance, one great single branch jutting towards the sky like a menacing spear—like the statue of the Archangel. Christina's lips moved in a silent prayer: 'Help me.'

And the door catch suddenly moved under her hand. The door was open, she realised, and she was struggling to hold it shut against the wind that tore at it. She was very calm, and she knew exactly what she was going to do. Theo was laughing softly to himself, driving straight at the tree. Just another target in this incredible game of 'chicken' he was playing, and at the last minute he would pull away again.

With her free hand, she lunged for the steering wheel, dragging at it so that the tree still lay directly in their careering path. Theo swore, a high startled sound, and she felt him brake violently. She pushed at the door which swung open and jumped for the undergrowth at the side of the road. Her body hit the ground with a sickening impact, and she rolled over in the grass and ferns and lay very still for a moment.

She moved at last very gingerly in case she had damaged herself, but she seemed to be all in one piece, although very bruised and shaken. She got slowly on to her knees and stared apprehensively at Theo's car. It had come to rest against the tree trunk, and part of the bonnet had smashed. There was no movement inside the car and after a moment she lifted herself stiffly on to her feet and went over to it.

Theo was sprawled over the driving wheel. For one terrible moment she thought he was dead, then her questing fingers found the strong pulse in his limply dangling hand and she realised with a flood of relief that he was still alive. He gave a slight groan and she stepped back, her reason telling her urgently that when he eventually came round, she would do well to be as far away as possible.

Half running, half stumbling, she forced her aching legs to carry her away from the car, her feet making no sound on the undergrowth. The wind tore at her viciously, whipping her tangled hair across her face. She didn't even know where she was running to, wasn't even sure which direction she had taken. Was she going towards Archangel, or back to

La Villette? She stopped to take a painful breath, her hand pressed to her side. She didn't even know how far they had come. At first, she had been too preoccupied to notice, and when Theo had started his 'game' all other considerations had been driven from her mind.

She began to trot again, regulating her breathing, forcing her leaden limbs to obey her, all her senses keyed up to hear above the crackle of thunder and the rising shriek of the wind, the distant sound of pursuit. He would come after her, she was sure, and he would be angry, and in his present mood, that anger might be unsafe. She shivered, realising a little for the first time what she had escaped by her refusal to marry him.

She glanced around her as she ran, looking for possible hiding places. She had no idea how badly the car was damaged. but it was possible that he might still be able to drive it. Had the headlights been smashed in the collision, or would they come flaring out of the gloom presently to pin her down like a moth caught in a flame?

It was some ten minutes later that she heard it. At first, she thought it was the growl of thunder, then she recognised the throb of an engine, not going fast, but coming her way. She looked round with swift desperation. He would be expecting her to run inland, across the fields, so she would go the other way.

She felt for the guard rail and lifted herself cautiously over it. Below her she could see the sea, sullenly tossing its white-capped waves. The surf didn't whisper today. It ground and tore at the beach with a hollow, booming sound, and she could feel the spray on her face. It was one of the most uninviting prospects she had ever seen, and for a moment she hesitated, then the wind died away suddenly and she heard the car engine again closer now and going steadily. She didn't wait any longer, but lowered herself over the edge. She had expected a sudden drop, but it was a steep slope covered in scrub, and she clutched gratefully at handfuls of it, praying that it would not give way under her weight. The wind grabbed and buffeted at her as if it was trying to pluck her from her precarious perch and send her sailing to the beach below, and she pressed herself closer to the cliff-face, trying to become part of the unyielding rock. Some of the fronds she was clutching at became dislodged and she slithered further down for one heart-stopping moment before she was able to grab a firmer hold. The car was just above her on the road now, its engine whining and sounding rough. It was going quite slowly. He was watching for her, and even though she knew that she was in the last place he would ever look, she became perfectly motionless and even held her breath until the noise of the labouring engine had passed and was gone, lost on the howling wind.

She relaxed suddenly, tremblingly, and slid a few more feet. If she did not take care she would reach a point where she could not climb up again. She stared up at the darkness above her, waiting for the next lightning flash to reveal where the cliff edge was. It seemed very far away, and although she knew it was the wrong thing to do, she turned herself gingerly and stared down into the seething blackness below.

For a moment, she thought she was imagining the gleam of light. That it was either wishful thinking, or more likely some weird reflection from what remained of Theo's headlights as he made his way down towards Archangel. But it did not vanish or flicker, but shone steadily on like a small beacon of hope. She stared down at it almost fiercely, trying to dismiss the sudden wild excitement rising within her. Was it really possible that she was closer to Archangel than she had ever suspected, and that the small glimmer of light was coming from Devlin's shack?

She made herself think calmly, and try to get her bearings. That day she had sprained her ankle, Devlin had been riding a horse on the beach. It had not gone back along the beach, which suggested there was another way to reach Archangel. A path—a usable track down this cliff. Usable by a horse, anyway—a horse which knew its way back to the stable, and where a horse could go, so could she.

She began to move slowly and carefully sideways towards the gleam of light. Occasionally she slipped, but now she let her body go with a strange confidence that the gradient would not betray her. Every move she made, she thought, was bringing her closer to Devlin—and safety. All the same, she could hardly believe it when her groping fingers no longer encountered the scrub and bushes she had relied on so far. There were stones, instead, pebbles and larger rocks which slipped and bounced away as she clutched at them. She heard them clatter down and knew with a surging relief that she had found the track at last.

Uncaring now of the pain in her bruised and scratched body, and the damage to her clothes, she let herself slide and scramble the few remaining feet to the beach below. The bulk of the shack was immediately in front of her, and she stumbled round to the door and hammered on it with her fists.

She suffered during the next few seconds of silence. Perhaps he had gone away and left the lamp burning. After all, the beach could not be the healthiest place in the world in a storm. Or maybe he was—not alone. And at that thought, none of the aches of her battered body could equal the pain in her heart.

She was about to turn away when the door swung open, and he stood there. For a moment his eyes travelled disbelievingly over her, then with a sound between a groan and a curse he pulled her towards him into the room, and closed the door, shutting them in together.

He held her by her shoulders, and when he spoke, there was controlled fury in his voice. 'What in hell have you been doing? Don't you know you should stay indoors in weather like this? This is a hurricane, you idiot girl, although we're only catching the edge of it, thank God. It's not some gentle English rainstorm to go walking in. And what's happened to you? You look as if you've fallen down a cliff.'

'I did,' she said unsteadily. 'At least, I didn't fall—I climbed down. Wasn't that clever of me?' She began to laugh, and recoiled, shocked into silence by his stinging slap across her cheek.

'Sit down.' He pushed her without gentleness towards the couch. 'I'll get you a drink and something for those scratches before they turn septic.'

'I don't want a drink.' Her eyes were wide and hostile as she put a hand to her face.

'Maybe not, but you need one—and so, incidentally, do I.' He walked abruptly across the room and disappeared into the sleeping area.

Christina relaxed gratefully into the cushions, her soreness relishing their comfort. The light she had seen came from a large lamp on the work bench where Devlin had obviously been occupied before she interrupted him. But how could anyone work on an evening like this? she asked herself, as the building shook under the impact of the wind. She remembered with a shiver the warning of the cheerful man in La Villette. *'Tie your roof on or the devil's breath will whistle it right into the sea.'*

Devlin returned, carrying a blue denim shirt over his arm. He tossed it at her. 'Wear this,' he directed briefly. 'It may not cover as much as you'd like, but at least it will be more decent than those rags you're wearing.'

Glancing down at herself, she saw for the first time what he meant, and the colour rose in her face. Her own jeans and top were nearly in shreds. Her hand went to what was left of the zip, then paused. Shouldn't she go into the bedroom to change, even though he had not suggested it? She gave him an uncertain glance and saw that his back was determinedly turned to her while he dealt with the bottles in a cabinet. And it was only really a matter of seconds to discard what she was wearing and slip into the shirt. It was buttoned, and she was rolling up the sleeves by the time he turned round with a glass in his hand. 'Here.'

She took a sip. It caught at the back of her throat and she choked a little, but there was a feeling like molten fire running along her veins. He gave her a sardonic grin. 'A concoction of Ludo Bellairs,' he explained. 'He's thinking of patenting it.'

'He should.' She sipped again, and then leaned back, closing her eyes.

'No, Christy.' She felt the studio couch give under his weight as he came to sit beside her. 'You can sleep later. Now, you've got to tell me what's happened.'

She opened her eyes unwillingly and stared at him. It would be far easier, she thought, just to shut her eyes and let the world simply drift away.

'You were right, you see,' she said slowly. 'She—your aunt—did intend to marry me to Theo. She said I could go —back to England. But it wasn't true. She was even having the ring—the Brandon ring—altered for me. Lorna Maynard told me. I—I ran away, to La Villette. But the boat to Martinique had been cancelled because of the storm and Theo found me and brought me back.' It was a disjointed account, but he seemed to have little difficulty in interpeting it.

'And where is Theo now?'

'Back at Archangel, I suppose.' She swallowed. 'He was playing one of his games with me—like he did in the swimming pool. Testing me out—seeing if I had enough spirit to be the bride of a Brandon.' She heard Devlin swear softly and hurried on. 'He was swerving the car from one side of the road to the other, going much too fast, pretending that we were going over the cliff. I grabbed the wheel and we crashed into a tree—not badly, but he was knocked out. I jumped clear and then I ran away. But he came after me, and I knew if I went across the plantation he'd see me, so I went over the cliff instead. And it—it just turned out to be this particular cliff, and I remembered the way the horse had gone—and came down.'

'Dear God,' he said. 'You must have a very potent guardian angel. Any other stretch and you'd probably have been killed.'

'I know.' She took another sip. 'And I do have a guardian —the Archangel himself. How odd that he should help me and not Theo. After all, he's the Brandon, not me.'

Devlin shook his head. 'No, Christy. Theo's no more a Brandon than you are. I don't know how much you're aware of in the family history, but you probably don't know that my uncle and Marcelle were childless. It was a great grief to him, but almost an obsession with her, made the more unbearable because her own sister, my mother, had the son she craved.' He lit a cheroot and drew on it deeply. 'By the time I was in my teens, Uncle Charles was resigned, I think, and it was understood that I was to inherit Archangel. I was at school then and finding out a few things, including the fact that just to be a Brandon of Archangel didn't necessarily mean you were a lord of creation. It seemed to me that the whole thing was questionable— morally and economically. The final straw, if you like, was having to live with the obscenity that my ancestors, my own flesh and blood, had actually owned slaves. That really did something to me. When I came home for the holidays I talked rather wildly about the changes I would make when Archangel was mine. It was bloody stupid of me, but I was only a kid. But as soon as I had gone back to school, Tante started to work on Uncle Charles. He was a Brandon to his fingertips in some ways and obviously I'd upset him. The next thing my parents knew she had produced Theo. She always claimed he was the orphaned son of some distant relatives of hers on Martinique, but it wasn't a relationship we

were ever able to trace. I imagine the only one who knows
the truth, apart from Tante herself, is Adèle Christophe,
and she's totally loyal to Tante, of course.'

'But she couldn't just make Theo the heir ...'

'She persuaded Uncle Charles to adopt him. He was a
very young child then, so they made no pretence of being
his parents. The polite fiction was that they were his grand-
parents. I don't think anyone really blamed them. He was a
beautiful-looking kid—quite irresistible even then. Anyone
would have wanted to adopt him. And there he was, young
and malleable, to be trained in the almighty Brandon tradition. With a suitable marriage to follow as soon as he was
old enough, just to ensure that I never got my evil des-
tructive hands on the sacred estate.' He stubbed out the
cheroot violently in an ashtray.

'It was then things started to go astray. People might not
blame Tante for wanting a child and taking her own steps
to acquire one, but it was a different matter when it was
found out he was the new heir. That was going too far,
dispossessing a real Brandon to put an imitation one in his
place.' He laughed shortly. 'Feudal, isn't it? But the family
have been at Archangel a long time, and compared with
some I suppose it's been a benevolent despotism. I think if
Uncle Charles had lived, he might have altered his will yet
again. He was clearly dissatisfied with the way Theo was
turning out. But he died, and my parents had also been
killed by then, so Tante was supreme. And in her eyes, her
darling boy could do not wrong. When the feelers she'd
been putting out about possible marriages were gently but
firmly declined—no one knew what his real background
might be—she decided to look further afield.'

'And she found me.' Christina stared down at her glass.
'Oh God—she found me!'

'Yes,' he said grimly. 'Someone who had learned to do as
she was told, and be grateful. The ideal candidate, to be
spoiled and flattered and nudged slowly but surely into

Theo's arms. Only you weren't like that. Under that docile exterior, there was an unexpectedly stubborn streak—and a temper. So Theo started to let you know about his hidden streak too . . .'

Reaction set in suddenly and she began to cry. Devlin's arms were swiftly about her, drawing her against him. For a moment she resisted, but the strength of his hands was too compelling, and she lay against him, sobbing helplessly. At the same moment, lightning lit up the room, to be succeeded almost at once by a deafening clap of thunder, and with a roar like an avalanche the rain began to fall.

It was what Christina first became aware of as she calmed again—that savage drumming on the roof of the shack, contrasting with the steady beat of his heart under her cheek and his hand gently and rhythmically stroking her hair. She sat upright, with a feeling of constraint, and moistened her lips slightly before she spoke. 'I—I'm sorry about that. I've made your shirt quite damp.'

His lips twitched slightly. 'It's still comparatively drier indoors than it would be out,' he said gravely. 'Now I'll see to those scratches of yours.'

'Oh, no.' Rather helplessly, she tugged his shirt over her knees. 'It's all right. Please don't bother.' It wasn't that the scratches didn't need attention. She knew, pitifully, that she could not answer for her response if he was to touch her again. The fact that another girl had a far greater claim on him than she did made no difference to the fact that she yearned to feel his mouth on hers. She was only too conscious of their isolation, cut off from the world in this shack while a storm raged outside.

'I—I hope you've got the roof tied on,' she said, striving for a light touch.

Devlin grinned and she knew he had picked up her reference. 'Oh, it won't get to that stage,' he said with casual confidence. 'This place has weathered worse blows than this. By morning it will all be over, you'll see.'

She started a little nervously. Was he meaning to imply that she would still be here in the morning? But that was impossible. She said nervously, 'I hope the rain eases soon. I shall have to be going . . .'

He leaned forward, placing a devastating finger on her parted lips. His silver eyes mocked her. 'You're going nowhere, Christy, my sweet. Here you are and here you'll stay until it's safe for you to leave.'

She jerked her head away. 'And is it so safe for me to stay?' she said in a low voice.

'You mean because there's only one bed?' He laughed, but there was no amusement in the sound. 'Well, as to that, we'll just have to wait and see. Unless you're issuing an invitation.'

'Don't—please,' she interrupted in a stifled voice.

'O.K.,' he returned savagely. 'But just don't provoke me, Christina. Now face the facts. If I allowed you to leave—in this weather, wearing nothing but one of my shirts—where would you go? To Archangel? You'd probably get a warm welcome. Everything forgiven and forgotten, back to square one. But if you stay the night here with me, you'd get a very different reception. You'd be packed off back to England, which is presumably what you want, so fast your feet wouldn't touch the ground. I'm poison to Tante, and if she thought you'd slept with me, you'd be the same. That's a betrayal she would never forgive, take my word for it.'

She knew he was right, but her heart quailed at the thought of spending a whole night with him in such intimate proximity. Did she have the ability or the strength to conceal the truth from him—to hide the longing that consumed her to be in his arms in the ultimate nearness of passion?

'I—I don't know what to say.' She pushed her hair nervously off her face, avoiding his glance unless he should read her thoughts in her eyes.

He swore suddenly and shockingly. 'What the hell do

you take me for?' he asked with dangerous softness. 'Some kind of sadist on Theo's lines? You've just-been through probably the worst day of your young life. You're frightened, you're hurt, physically and mentally, and you're tired, and yet you still have it in your head that in spite of all this I'm going to force myself on you. Dear God!' He pushed his hand wearily through his tawny hair.

'I'm sorry——' she began awkwardly, but he flung up a hand to silence her and she saw the mockery was back in his eyes.

'Oh, my motives aren't entirely chivalrous, I assure you. I want you, and under any other circumstances, I'd take you —and make you want me too. But it seems that every time we meet, you're either injured or needing some kind of help. I'm getting a little tired of being a protector to you, Christina. I have this—fantasy where you're coming across the beach. The sun's shining, and you're shining too, all the shadows gone and all wounds healed. And you're coming to me, not because you need help or comfort, but because you need me in the way a woman should need a man. And you come up those steps into my arms, and that's where you stay because that's where you want to be.'

His voice had dropped huskily, and the colour flamed in her cheeks at the image his words had produced in her mind.

Somehow she forced herself to shrug, uneasily aware at the same time that the gesture made the shirt slip revealingly from one bare shoulder.

'But you said yourself—didn't you—that it was only a fantasy. You don't really expect it to come true?'

'You'd be amazed at some of my expectations,' he said softly. 'Now, I advise you to make yourself scarce into the other room and get some rest before that—garment you're wearing slips any further and I decide to forget my good intentions and—er—reclaim my property. Scat!'

She obeyed without demur, climbing into the wide bed

and huddling the covers around her with a shiver as the wind caught the shack again, worrying it like a terrier before the gust died away. If this was only the edge of a hurricane, what must it be like when they were really caught by one? she wondered apprehensively, and hoped she would never find out.

Her eyes widened as Devlin came through the bead curtain. He was carrying a bowl of water, some cotton wool and a tube of antiseptic which he placed beside the bed.

'Here,' he said curtly. 'Under the circumstances, I think you'd better attend to your scratches yourself. Watch out for that stuff, it stings.'

He was right, she discovered, wincing. She slipped the shirt off altogether and examined herself ruefully. She would be black and blue by morning, and there were ugly grazes on her arms and legs. Her back hurt too, but she could not reach the spot herself no matter how she squirmed, and she dared not call Devlin.

She replaced the cap on the tube of cream, and lay down again. She felt very bleak suddenly. Devlin's fantasy had made a potent appeal to her senses which she now had to exorcise before it was too late. She must not forget she would not be the first to succumb to his overwhelming attraction and the blatant temptation he offered.

She wondered what he was doing in the other room. He was certainly very quiet, she thought, straining her ears for a sound of movement. Perhaps he had gone back to the work she had interrupted by her arrival. He had said he was getting ready for an exhibition, and he must have work to finish—Eulalie's statuette among them. She turned on to her stomach, burying her face in the pillow. It was unbearable to think of him touching the figure, she thought, smoothing it down, rediscovering all the voluptuous curves that were already so familiar to him in warm, rounded flesh rather than hard wood.

She stirred uneasily, only too aware of the fact that he

had probably shared this very bed with Eulalie. It was this kind of realisation that would have to be her safeguard, she told herself, biting savagely at her lip. She didn't want to be just another woman in Devlin's life, taken and discarded as the whim seized him.

In spite of her disturbed thoughts, she found her physical fatigue was beginning to get the better of her, and she kept sinking into a light doze, to wake with a thumping heart and dry mouth when a more than ordinarily fierce gust hit the building. The rain was as heavy as ever, but the lightning seemed to be lessening, and there was longer and longer between each roll of thunder, making her think the storm might be passing over.

She had almost lulled herself off to sleep with this consoling thought when an almighty crash brought her bolt upright, the answering scream she could not control already on her lips.

Devlin came into the room. He looked tired and angry. 'For God's sake,' he said irritably. 'It's only a bloody shutter.'

His eyes went over her, widening, and she realised, too late, what a spectacle she must present. Hurriedly she scooped the covers up to her throat.

'Thank you,' he said with too-elaborate courtesy. 'Things are quite difficult enough without you flashing yourself at me like some tart from a girlie magazine.'

She gasped and her face flamed. 'That's a lousy thing to say!'

'Well, I happen to feel lousy.'

'And so do I,' she flared back at him. 'You said it yourself, remember? I'm frightened, I'm hurt and I'm tired, but principally I'm frightened. This may be just another storm to you, but it isn't to me. Every time I close my eyes I'm afraid the next time I open them there won't be four walls round me. I didn't know that crash was just—a bloody shutter. And if I hadn't screamed you wouldn't even have come in here to see if I was all right.'

His lean body had gone very rigid. 'No, I wouldn't,' he said in a low voice. 'You may look young, Christy, but you're surely woman enough to know why I'm keeping away. Don't you know what it does to me to know that you're in here, in my bed, only a few feet away from me?'

Her voice trembled. 'Oh, yes, I know. And it can't be any worse than what the same knowledge does to me.'

His eyes narrowed unbelievingly for a moment, then he took a step forward. His hands were already unfastening his shirt. 'I see,' he said very softly. 'Well, in that case ...'

Christina closed her eyes and kept them resolutely shut even when the bed beside her yielded to his weight. When he reached for her, his hands were gentle.

'Oh, Christy,' there was a note of laughter in his husky voice, mingled with an amazing tenderness, 'have you any idea how good—how incredibly good—you feel?'

'So do you,' she managed out of a dry throat.

'So my touch isn't still abhorrent to you?' he questioned gravely, and her eyes flew open, startled, to search his face. He laughed again, deep in his throat, then bent to claim her mouth with passionate possessiveness.

She clung to him unashamedly, responding with every fibre of her being. No rain, no hurricane wind could compare with this storm of desire Devlin could create in her— was creating in her. And yet, even as she abandoned herself to the breathless languor that his caresses were inducing, she sensed that something was amiss. The storm seemed to be getting louder at every minute. The pounding of the rain on the roof seemed almost to be in the room with them.

'Dear God in heaven!' Devlin lifted himself away from her and sat up, listening intently. 'There's someone at the door.' He gave a muffled groan. 'Surely there can't be more of Theo's bloody victims demanding sanctuary?'

He threw himself out of bed and dragged on his jeans, fastening them as he went out of the room.

Christina could hear it now properly, the desperate banging on the door. It didn't seem likely, but she supposed it could be just another refugee from the storm.

Above the howl of the wind, she heard the door open and Devlin's voice sounding surprised. And then she heard another voice she recognised, speaking urgently. It was Clive Maynard.

Devlin strode back into the bedroom, picking up his shirt and thrusting his arms into it.

'I have to go up to Archangel,' he said. 'Clive's come for me. There's been an accident.'

'Is it Mrs Brandon?' Christina lifted herself on to her elbow and stared at him. 'She was ill yesterday—a heart attack of some kind. Should I come with you?'

He considered rapidly, then nodded. 'It might be best. I don't know how long I'll be, and you'd only scare yourself into hysterics if you were here for hours by yourself.' He went over to the clothes cupboard and took out a light waterproof coat which he tossed on to the bed. 'It'll swamp you, but it will have to do. Hurry!'

She obeyed him, her hands shaking. It was only when she was enveloped in the folds of coat and coming out of the bedroom that she remembered she had Clive Maynard to face. She coloured painfully as she met his gaze, but he just said, 'Oh, hullo, Christina,' as if her presence was entirely natural. She supposed it was not the first time that he had come to summon Devlin and found him with a woman, and bit her lip.

Devlin was standing by the door, rocking impatiently on his toes. He took her arm, gripping it tightly. 'It's the track again, I'm afraid, honey girl. Clive has the Range Rover waiting at the top. And don't look so scared. The wind isn't nearly as bad as it was.'

But it was bad enough, she thought, as she scrambled up the track again, bent and almost on all fours. She was gasping for breath when she reached the top and the comparative shelter of the Range Rover. She sat between Clive and Devlin in the front seat and Devlin drove.

'Where did it happen?' he flung at Clive across the top of her head.

Clive passed a hand wearily across his eyes. 'At the gates,' he answered. 'They were fastened open, of course, but the wind must have dislodged one of them and it blew across, just at that moment. He must have been going at a hell of a lick—and he'd already had one smash-up, by all accounts. He hit the gate head-on—wouldn't have stood a chance. The phone's out of order, of course, but Louis has gone for the doctor—not that there's anything he can do.'

'No,' Devlin said quietly, and Christina saw that his face was taut under his tan.

She touched his arm timidly. 'What's happened? Is—is it Theo?'

'Yes,' he said, and was silent as the Range Rover turned off the road towards the enormous wrought iron gates which marked the entrance to Archangel. One of them was still half across, supporting the tangled mass of metal which had once been a car. Christina stifled a gasp as she saw it, and Clive put an arm round her shoulders and gave her a comforting squeeze. 'Don't look,' he suggested gently.

All the lights were on in the house, and Madame Christophe stood at the top of the steps as she had done when Christina first arrived there, watching for them coming. But this time she came hurrying down, her normally impassive face working. 'Ah, M'sieur Devlin.' She clutched at him as he climbed out of the vehicle. '*Le pauvre petit!* Thank heaven you have come. Madame is distraught—beside herself.'

'Yes.' He disengaged himself gently enough and put her from him. 'Where have they put him, Adèle?'

'In his room. I myself have done what was necessary. To think that I should have to do such a thing ...' Her face puckered as if she was going to burst into tears.

Devlin spoke sharply. 'There will have to be an inquest,

of course. That can't be avoided, even by my aunt. How did it happen, have you any idea?'

She shrugged. 'He came home in a temper,' she said tonelessly. 'The car was damaged and he spoke of an accident. Then he demanded M'mselle.' Her eyes went past Devlin to where Christina stood by the Range Rover. 'When he discovered she had not returned, he became angry—violent. He said he knew where she had run to and he would fetch her back by her hair. Madame tried to remonstrate with him, to calm him—but he struck her and ran out to the car again. We heard him go down the drive—there was something wrong with the engine and he was shouting at the top of his voice—screaming curses. Then, seconds later, we heard the crash. Louis and I both ran, but it was too late.' She gave a long shuddering sigh. 'He was such a beautiful child. I saw him born and he was truly—exquisite. And when the dark mood was not on him, he could be very loving.'

He nodded. 'Go back to my aunt, Adèle, and tell her I will be with her presently.'

He watched her mount the steps and then came back with long strides to the Range Rover. He took Christina in his arms and kissed her mouth briefly and fiercely. He said, 'You see how things are here. Don't stay at the house tonight. Clive and Lorna will put you up, and I'll see you in the morning. I'd better warn you now, I intend to ask you to marry me.' He lifted her hand to his lips and turned away.

Clive touched her arm. 'Come on, Christina. Lorna will be so thankful to see you. She's been torturing herself ever since you left, thinking of you caught in La Villette in this storm. This—happening, I'm afraid, put everything else out of our minds, or we'd have sent out a search party for you.'

'It's all right,' she said. She lifted the hand Devlin had kissed and cherished it against her cheek. 'I was quite safe.'

She watched Devlin stride up the steps, his dark figure outlined against the light that streamed from the doorway. The wind had lessened now. It was only a shadow of what it had been an hour before. The rain too seemed to have spent itself and towards the sea the sky even appeared to be clearing a little. The devil's breath had blown, but only Theo had been the sufferer in the end. And she could even think with pity of the sick white-haired woman who waited in the great house with all her schemes in ruins about her. Devlin was master of Archangel now.

As Devlin reached the doorway, Eulalie suddenly appeared from within. Christina saw her head tilt as she looked up at him, her lips moving passionately. She saw Devlin shake his head and step forward, as if to pass her, and she saw Eulalie catch at his arm, her other hand pressed against her abdomen in a gesture more eloquent than any words could be. Devlin paused, then slowly, and it seemed to the paralysed girl in the shadow of the Range Rover reluctantly, he took her in his arms, cradling her dark head against his chest.

Christina turned away. 'Shall we go?' she said mechanically.

Her eyes were burning as the vehicle turned out of the drive and headed towards Clive's bungalow, but she did not cry. She thought she had shed all her tears in Devlin's arms at the beach house. But she must not think of Devlin's arms—or indeed of Devlin at all, and especially she must not think of those few abrupt words which had seemed so deliriously like a proposal of marriage. He owed her nothing. He had not even seduced her, and he owed Eulalie everything. She pressed her hand convulsively over her mouth to stifle a sob and sensed Clive was looking at her.

She marshalled all her efforts to ask him, 'What will she do now?'

He understood immediately that she was referring to Marcelle Brandon.

'Go back to Martinique, I suppose. She has some relatives there. She certainly won't want to stick round here and watch Devlin starting to dismantle the mighty Brandon edifice. I imagine she'll stay for the funeral, and then quietly vanish.' He gave her a sharp glance. 'Are you all right, Christina? You're awfully white. Not surprising, I suppose, really, but do tell me if you're going to be sick. I can always stop, you know . . .'

She gave him a travesty of a smile. 'I'm fine, really. I— I'm sorry I worried Lorna.'

There was silence between them until the bungalow was reached and Lorna came out to greet them. Her brows rose slightly when she saw what Christina was wearing, but she tactfully made no comment, merely shepherding her to the spare room and bringing her cases to her.

She thanked Lorna, refused all offers of supper and a warm drink, and when the door finally closed behind her hostess, fell across the bed and lay like a stone.

She awoke the following morning to a blaze of sunlight, and lay for a moment assimilating her surroundings and letting her memories of the previous day return slowly.

The door opened to admit Lorna with a cup of coffee. 'You're looking better for your sleep. We've all been tiptoeing round, trying not to disturb you. Drink this and then I'll send your visitor in.'

Christina paused in the act of raising the cup to her lips. 'Visitor?' she echoed.

Lorna winked wickedly at her. 'The new master,' she said in a stage whisper. 'I'm not devoted to the living room carpet, but he's been tramping up and down on it for almost an hour now, and it'll be worn out if he goes on much longer.'

Christina set her coffee down untasted. Her mouth was so dry she doubted whether she could have swallowed even a mouthful.

She said, and her voice sounded very young and breathless, 'I can't see him, Lorna. Please ask him to go.'

Lorna fixed her with a frankly incredulous stare. 'My dear girl, are you quite mad? Clive didn't mean to eavesdrop last night, but he was standing right next to you when Dev was speaking. He couldn't help overhearing. And—forgive me—you were—with him last night, weren't you?'

Christina swallowed. 'Yes—yes. But it didn't mean anything.' She tried an unconvincing laugh. 'You—you know how Devlin is . . .' Her voice tailed away.

Lorna gave her a disapproving stare. 'I know how he was,' she emphasised. And he hasn't been a saint, I'll grant you that. But he's never proposed marriage to one of his fancies before—and in front of witnesses, to boot. So it must have meant something to him.'

Christina bent her head. 'At the time, maybe,' she said. 'But it's daylight now and, as you said, he's the new master. He has other things on his mind, other responsibilities.' In spite of all she could do, an image of Eulalie rose in her mind.

'Hm.' Lorna was clearly unimpressed. 'And yet he's here, isn't he?' She got up purposefully. 'If you're not going to drink that coffee, I think I'll just tell him to come on in and argue with you himself.'

'No!' Christina caught frantically at her hand. 'Please, Lorna. I do mean it—I don't want to see him again. Tell him I'm ill. Tell him anything you like, but make him go away. Please!'

Lorna gave a defeated little shrug. 'If that's really what you want,' she said quietly.

'It is.' Christina was adamant, clinging to her hand.

'Very well.' Lorna freed herself from her grip. 'But it isn't a task I relish.'

After she had gone, Christina got out of bed and padded across to the door. There was a bolt on it, and she pushed it across with trembling fingers—a second line of defence in case Lorna's persuasions failed.

But it wasn't needed. A few seconds ticked by in silence,

then she heard swift steps going away down the passage to the front door, and the door slam. A moment later a car engine started up with an unnecessary amount of revving, and drove away.

She went slowly back to the bed and sank down on it, her legs trembling too much to support her any longer. That, she told herself, is that.


She did not attend the inquest on Theo which opened the following day in Fort Victoire, but stayed quietly at the bungalow with Lorna and the children. When Clive returned, he said a verdict of accidental death had been returned, and that Marcelle Brandon had looked like death herself while she was giving evidence.

'Is she going back to Martinique?' Lorna asked, deftly cutting up fruit for a salad.

'Yes, immediately after the funeral tomorrow. Adèle Christophe is going with her, and the girl Eulalie, poor creature.'

'I don't know why you say that,' Lorna exclaimed. 'She was an obnoxious girl, I always thought.'

Christina laid down the fruit knife she was using, and listened, her heart thumping.

'I thought so too, but there was one person she appealed to, apparently—the late Master Theo. It seems they'd been having a full-blooded affair for months. She had some delusion that he'd marry her—even wheedled Devlin into carving a damned figure of herself to give him for his birthday. Seems she thought the gift would bind him to her in some way. Madness, of course. He never would have married her, baby or no baby.'

'You mean she's pregnant?' Lorna queried, flabbergasted.

He nodded. 'About three or four months. Adèle has been trying to persuade her not to go to the funeral, but she's quite determined. She wants the figure Devlin carved to be buried with Theo.'

Lorna grimaced, then turned hurriedly to Christina, who had given a little cry.

'What's wrong, love? Have you cut yourself? Let me see.'

'No—no, really,' Christina assured her, spreading out her fingers so that Lorna could check they were all intact. She smiled beatifically at the two astonished faces confronting her. 'Can you manage without me for a while? There—there's someone I have to see.'

She was breathless by the time she got to the cove, and she slowed her pace deliberately as she walked across the yielding sand towards the beach house.

All the time, the fear nagged at her that he might not be there. That he might have already moved out and gone up to Archangel to live. The thought of seeking him out there was a daunting one.

But as she approached, she saw a movement and Devlin came round the corner of the shack carrying a hammer and some other implements. When he saw her, he bent and put them down on the verandah, then straightened and watched her come towards him, his hands resting lightly on his hips. He looked older, and tired, and there was a grimness about his face which made her steps falter a little, but she kept going to the foot of the verandah, and looked up at him.

'Hello, Christy.' His voice was cool and pleasant, and gave no indication as to his feelings. He might have been addressing any chance-come caller. When she did not answer, he went on, 'Was there something you wanted?'

'Yes.' She moistened her lips. 'I want you.'

He did not speak, nor did he move towards her, and after a moment she hurried on, 'And I'm not injured in any way and I'm not just looking for a refuge—or a protector. I've come just as you wanted me to—because I need you.'

'No shadows?' The silver eyes watched her steadily. 'That was also one of the conditions.'

'Not any more,' she said. 'Oh, Devlin, I've been such a fool!'

'Everyone's entitled to be that occasionally,' he said, and smiled. In his smile she saw that incredible tenderness again, and her heart lifted and sang because everything was suddenly, miraculously all right. 'Come here.' He held out his arms to her compellingly. 'I've got to hold you to know that you're real, and not just another fantasy.'

She ran to him then, lifting her face almost blindly for his kiss. As he swung her up into his arms and turned towards the doorway, she checked him. 'Dev—darling, I must explain ...'

'Not now,' he kissed her again, parting her lips with an arrogance that devastated her. 'Later—much later. Save the explanations for our honeymoon when we run out of things to discuss.'

'We—we are going to be married?' The look in his eyes was filling her with sudden shyness as well as a secret throbbing delight.

'Oh yes,' he said calmly. 'Just as soon as I can arrange it. After all, we don't want to let my mother and your Aunt Grace down, do we?' He grinned down at her flushed face. 'Oh, I knew it, my sweet one—the plans they'd made. I'd even wondered what you were like, at times. What stuck in my throat was when you turned up at Archangel, destined for Theo, and I discovered who you were. So you do appreciate, I hope, just why I don't intend to let you out of my sight from now on, day or night?'

She smiled, her long lashes veiling her eyes. 'Whatever you say, Mr Brandon, sir,' she murmured. 'But Devlin, I do wish you'd let me explain ...'

'Later, honey girl,' he said against her lips. 'Afterwards.'

He carried her into the shack and kicked the door shut behind them.

# ROMANCE

## Variety is the spice of romance

Each month, Mills & Boon publish new romances. New stories about people falling in love. A world of variety in romance — from the best writers in the romantic world. Choose from these titles in September.

**BOND OF VENGEANCE** Jessica Steele
**CALIFORNIA DREAMING** Sara Francis
**SWEET TEMPEST** Helen Bianchin
**LEGALLY BOUND** Kerry Allyne
**THE PASSIONATE ESCAPE** Mary Lyons
**A NAKED FLAME** Charlotte Lamb
**TOO FAR, TOO FAST** Elizabeth Oldfield
**YEAR'S HAPPY ENDING** Betty Neels
**VIKING INVADER** Sally Wentworth
**WANTING** Penny Jordan
**ONCE A LOVER** Claire Harrison
**RUN SO FAR** Peggy Nicholson

On sale where you buy paperbacks. If you require further information or have any difficulty obtaining them, write to: Mills & Boon Reader Service, PO Box 236, Thornton Road, Croydon, Surrey CR9 3RU, England.

## Mills & Boon
## the rose of romance

# Mills & Boon

# Accept 4
# Best Selling Romances
# Absolutely
# FREE

Enjoy the very best of love, romance and intrigue brought to you by Mills & Boon. Every month Mills & Boon very carefully select 4 Romances that have been particularly popular in the past and re-issue them for the benefit of readers who may have missed them first time round. Become a subscriber and you can receive all 4 superb novels every month, and your personal membership card will entitle you to a whole range of special benefits too: a free monthly newsletter, packed with exclusive book offers, recipes, competitions and your guide to the stars, plus there are other bargain offers and big cash savings.

**AND an Introductory FREE GIFT for YOU.
Turn over the page for details.**

As a special introduction we will send you
FOUR superb and exciting
Best Seller Romances – yours to keep Free
– when you complete and return
this coupon to us.

At the same time we will reserve a
subscription to Mills & Boon Best Seller
Romances for you. Every month you will
receive the 4 specially selected Best Seller
novels delivered direct to your door. Postage
and packing is always completely Free.
There is no obligation or commitment -
you can cancel your subscription
at any time.

You have absolutely nothing to lose and a whole world of
romance to gain. Simply fill in and post the coupon today to:-
MILLS & BOON READER SERVICE, FREEPOST,
P.O. BOX 236, CROYDON, SURREY CR9 9EL.

Please note:– READERS IN SOUTH AFRICA write to
Mills & Boon Ltd., Postbag X3010,
Randburg 2125, S. Africa.

- - - - - - - - - - - - - - - - - - - - - - - - - - - - -

# FREE BOOKS CERTIFICATE

**To: Mills & Boon Reader Service, FREEPOST, P.O. Box 236,
Croydon, Surrey CR9 9EL.**

Please send me, free and without obligation, four Mills & Boon Best Seller Romances, &
reserve a Reader Service Subscription for me. If I decide to subscribe I shall receive four new
books each month for £4.00, post and packing free. If I decide not to subscribe, I shall write
to you within 10 days. The free books are mine to keep in any case. I understand that I may
cancel my subscription at any time simply by writing to you. I am over 18 years of age.
*Please write in BLOCK CAPITALS.*

Name _____

Address _____

_____

_____ Postcode _____

**SEND NO MONEY — TAKE NO RISKS.**
*Remember, postcodes speed delivery  Offer applies in UK only and is not valid to
present subscribers. Mills & Boon reserve the right to exercise discretion
in granting membership  If price changes are necessary you will be noti-
fied. Offer expires 31st December 1984.*

4BS

EP10B